The Tex

STAND-ALONE NOVEL

A Western Historical Adventure Book

by

Zachary McCrae

Disclaimer & Copyright

This is a work of fiction. Names, characters, places, and incidents are either products of the author's imagination or are used fictitiously. Any resemblance to actual events, locales, or persons, living or dead, is entirely coincidental.

Copyright © 2025 by Zachary McCrae

All Rights Reserved.

No part of this book may be reproduced, duplicated, transmitted, or recorded in any form—electronic or printed—without the prior written permission of the publisher. Unauthorized storage or distribution of this document is strictly prohibited.

Table of Contents

The Texas Blizzard ...**Error! Bookmark not defined.**
   Disclaimer & Copyright 2
   Table of Contents 3
   Letter from Zachary McCrae 5
Prologue 6
Chapter One 12
Chapter Two 21
Chapter Three 29
Chapter Four 37
Chapter Five 46
Chapter Six 55
Chapter Seven 64
Chapter Eight 72
Chapter Nine 80
Chapter Ten 88
Chapter Eleven 96
Chapter Twelve 105
Chapter Thirteen 113
Chapter Fourteen 121
Chapter Fifteen 129
Chapter Sixteen 137
Chapter Seventeen 145
Chapter Eighteen 152
Chapter Nineteen 160

Chapter Twenty 169
Chapter Twenty-One.. 177
Chapter Twenty-Two.. 185
Chapter Twenty-Three 193
Chapter Twenty-Four... 201
Chapter Twenty-Five.. 211
Chapter Twenty-Six 219
Chapter Twenty-Seven 226
Epilogue 236
   Also by Zachary McCrae 245

Letter from Zachary McCrae

I'm a man who loves plain things: a cup of strong coffee in the morning, a good book at noon, and my wife's embrace at night.

I want to write stories that take you by the hand and show you what it meant to be someone who tried to make ends meet and find their own way in the 19th-century United States. I've been this someone for a long time in my life, always looking for my next gig after my parents' sudden death, always finding new friends, but somehow not being able to stick with 'em. It's easy to find quantity in your life, but what about quality?

At the age of 50, and after my baby boy, Jeb, and my sweet daughter, Janette, went away to study East, with my sweet wife, Mrs. Maryanne McCrae, we moved back to my hometown and my dad's ranch close to the Rockies. After a series of health issues that have brought me even closer to our Lord, I've officially started writing those stories I always loved to read.

I'm tending my land and animals now with the help of Maryanne, and I'm grateful for each day I get to walk in this world we call Earth. As the saying goes, "Nature gave us all something to fall back on, and sooner or later we all land flat on it," so I want to take care of it just the way it has taken care of my dad and mom, and my cousins.

My adventure stories are my legacy to my children and to all of the readers who will honor me by following my work. God bless you and your families and our land! Thank you.

Stay safe but adventurous,

Zachary McCrae

Prologue

Hollister Ranch, Near Sherman, Texas — 1853

Pa always said that sweat was a prayer the land understood, and Tate took that as gospel.

So, no matter how much the splintered wood chafed his palm, he dug on. Another fence post set, another yard of wire to string. As sweat trickled down his temples, carving paths through the dust caked on his skin, his muscles burned with the strain of good, honest work.

"Hey, Tate." Wyatt hammered a post next to Tate. "Bet you five cents I can spit farther than you from the top of that there ridge."

"You ain't got five cents."

"Do, too—found it in the pocket of Pa's old coat. He said I could have it." Wyatt stretched his lanky limbs and leaned against the newly set post. "What do you say? You chicken?"

Tate laughed. "I know better than to take a bet from you. You'll find some way to cheat."

"Fine—I've got something better, anyway." Wyatt's unruly hair, the color of bleached straw, drank in the sunlight as the wind tousled it. "Pa brought in a new stallion yesterday. Real beauty, black as night."

Tate straightened and loosened his broad shoulders. "Black, you say?"

Wyatt nodded. "With a little white star on his forehead. Pa's calling him Midnight. Want to see him?"

"Unless you can convince a sucker to finish this fence, ain't no way."

"C'mon, your pa won't mind if you're gone a minute. Chore ain't goin' nowhere."

Tate frowned and pinched his lower lip.

Pa was out clearing the south pasture and wouldn't bother to check on Tate until the afternoon, anyway—maybe later, if Ma needed help with the baby.

A few minutes won't hurt.

He'd just pop off to Wyatt's, see the horse, and come straight back. Tate's face had been in the dirt all morning, and the sight of fence was starting to prick his skin.

Tate dropped his hammer. "Alright—but just for a minute."

As they scrambled onto Sunflower, Wyatt's swaybacked mare, Tate frowned; the poor beast really shouldn't carry more than one, but Pa's Saddlebred only left the stable for work, and Tate had gotten a smack upside his head the one time he'd snuck him out.

Sunflower would have to do.

Wyatt kicked her into a trot. "Heard Pa and Ma talkin' last night."

"Yeah? What about?"

"Pa says the Comanche are getting bolder. Hit a wagon train two days east of here."

Tate's gut twisted. "Pa and the other ranchers'll handle it."

"Reckon you're right." Wyatt shrugged. "It's all grown-up business, anyway."

Yeah, we ain't got nothin' to worry about.

Their fathers and the other ranchers worked the land, bending it to their will. What could a handful of Comanche do against men like that? No, all Tate had to worry about was seeing Midnight and rushing back before Pa caught him skipping out on chores.

Midnight was absolutely worth the hassle.

He stood proudly in his corral, all muscle and sinew, his coat drinking the sunlight. Oh, if only Tate had a horse like that! He'd ride across the plains, choose his own destiny beyond anything Pa could ever build for him.

Too soon, though, the thought of his abandoned chores broke into his little fantasy.

"I gotta get back. Pa will have my hide."

"Take Sunflower." Wyatt winked at him. "I'll come by later to get her."

Tate nodded and swung himself back onto the mare for the short ride home, imagining the scent of Ma's stew. He still had a lot to do before he could call it a day, but once he did, that savory—

Suddenly, a thick, acrid smell punched his nostrils.

The *wrong* scent.

Smoke...?

Smoke had no business coming from the direction of his house.

He pulled the mare to a halt at the edge of his family's spread; someone had trampled the fence he'd just raised, shattering the posts like matchsticks. Fighting his rising panic, he spurred Sunflower on, rushing to the cabin—only to find the door ripped off its hinges, the windows smashed, and the roof caved in.

No. This isn't right. This can't... I—

A shriek interrupted Tate's thoughts.

In the doorway, a soldier in a dusty blue coat with a brown beard and thick eyebrows cradled Tate's ma. In one arm, she clutched the swaddled form of his baby sister, Sarah.

Ma screamed as something dark seeped from her belly and onto the floorboards beneath her, staring at Sarah's crimson swaddling with tears in her—

Wait... Crimson swaddling...?

Tate jumped from Sunflower's back and collapsed to his knees in front of the cabin steps. Opening his mouth, he tried to shout, to call for help, then choked as he swallowed a gulp of smog-filled air.

Ma held Sarah tighter, her eyes fluttering closed.

Finding his voice, Tate screamed at the sky.

She'd been right there, and he hadn't even said goodbye. He'd wasted his chance to tell her he'd loved her. His last chance. Some son he was—some *brother*—dreaming of horses and freedom while someone killed his baby sister.

Tate looked around, his eyes feeling swollen and raw, as though filled with sand.

Pa lay by the woodpile where he and Tate had spent countless hours splitting firewood, arrows jutting from his torso, head, and throat. His pa—the man who'd been Tate's whole world—just... gone.

Why?

They'd been *good* people. Prayed every night. Ma had read from the Good Book, talking about a God who provided a fortress, a shield for the righteous.

Where are you now, Lord? Where's your shield?

It had been a lie—all of it—a monstrous, cruel lie told to make little ones sleep better at night. Tate had let himself get carried away, still thinking himself one of those little ones, trading work for foolish daydreams.

I should've been here—even if it meant dying with the rest of them.

Tate glared at the ground as the soldier approached and pulled him, unresisting, into a rough hug.

Hatred welled up within Tate, fueled by anger at the people who'd done this. He knew even before the soldier told him; the arrows in Pa's back revealed more than enough.

If God is good, a plague will strike them all down!

It wouldn't, of course. God had watched Tate's family die and done nothing. Tate had no reason to hope the 'good' Lord would lift a finger now.

As Tate trembled, staring at the red-stained floorboards, the soldier shook him, yelling; finally, several slaps stung Tate's cheek.

"Tate!"

Tate blinked. *Wyatt?*

"Tate—snap out of it!"

A lifetime ago, Tate might've answered. Now…

What's the point?

Then, a hand clamped down on his shoulder and spun him around, and Tate fell into Wyatt's arms.

"They hit us too." Wyatt sobbed. "Everyone. The whole settlement. They—they got Jacob."

Wyatt's older brother.

Of *course* it hadn't ended with Sarah, Ma, and Pa.

Why, God? Sarah and Jacob didn't deserve to die!

***

After everything, the Boone family took Tate in. Wyatt's parents seemed to have aged a decade in a single afternoon, yet for some reason, they still thanked God that Tate had survived.

That night, lying on Jacob's bed in Wyatt's room, Tate stared into the darkness. Once Wyatt had snapped him out of his stupor, the soldier had dragged Tate away, saying he "*shouldn't be watchin' this*" and, "*We'll dig them proper graves, don't you worry.*"

No matter what the soldier said, Tate resolved to go see his family as soon as he could sneak away. He knew he'd never feel anything close to peace if he didn't pay his respects.

Chapter One

Confederate Camp, Fairfax County, Virginia — 1861

Nine years later

Tate gagged on the taste of gunpowder; its acrid stench filled his nose, its bitter tang coating his tongue. Virginia mud, slick with rain and blood, sucked at his boots as he struggled to make sense of the cacophony.

The high-pitched whine of Minié balls parted the air. Guttural shouts ripped from the throats of men. The wet *thud* of lead piercing flesh repeated endlessly.

He wouldn't let the chaos get the better of him.

Not today.

Slamming another cartridge down the barrel of his Enfield, he blinked away the sweat stinging his eyes. *Fire. Reload. Fire. Again.* Only the rhythm mattered.

At this point, Tate had forgotten any prayer other than begging for his bullets to find their marks.

Though why he prayed in the first place, he had no idea.

To Tate's right, Wyatt worked his rifle with a smile on his angular face. The war had chiseled away all his baby fat and left behind harsh lines and a man who'd known too little food and too much hardship.

Lord knew he'd complained about it enough.

"Damn Yanks couldn't wait 'til a man's had his coffee!" Wyatt griped, reloading. "My gut's growlin' louder than this here rifle!"

Tate snickered. "And here I was, thinkin' you wouldn't be—"

Thump.

A force like a blacksmith's hammer slammed into Tate's left shoulder. Having never been hit before, Tate expected it to sting worse than a hornet, but it didn't—not at first, anyway—just a violent shove that spun him half around, his rifle tumbling into the mud. His arm numbed and went slack, a useless weight of meat and bone.

His vision blurred at the edges.

"Stay put, Tate—I'll hold 'em off!"

As Tate fumbled for his Remington pistol—he'd never trusted Colt's open frame design—Wyatt moved in front of him and fired without stopping.

Tate groaned. "Wyatt, get down, dagnabbit!"

"Get your head down, and be quiet!"

"I ain't worth the lead, you stubborn—"

"*Shut* it!"

Growling, Tate ripped the Remington from its holster. The Bluebellies were now focused on Wyatt, who'd grown tall as a scarecrow and just as conspicuous. Tate had to do *something* before someone managed to—

A puff of smoke erupted from the tree line.

Maybe because it didn't hit Tate, this shot didn't land so loudly, but with the soft *whump* of a distant axe splitting a log… as if Tate was back on the ranch, preparing firewood for the winter with Pa, and a Billy Yank hadn't just shot Wyatt.

Yet a wound opened on Wyatt's chest: a dark circle, no bigger than a coin—much smaller than Tate would've expected—blossoming on Wyatt's uniform and turning light-gray dark... about to take Tate's brother from him.

Wyatt's rifle slipped from his grasp. His smile vanished, and he blinked. His eyes, the clear blue of the Texas sky, found Tate's.

He opened his mouth, and, for a moment, Tate expected him to laugh and move on with the battle.

Instead, a gurgle pushed blood from his lips as he fell.

"Wyatt!" Tate caught him, then cradled Wyatt's head in his lap. "Look at me!"

A thin trickle of blood flowing from the corner of his mouth, Wyatt's lips moved again, but only a warble emerged.

Tate leaned in on the slim chance that maybe, just maybe, he'd catch a word or two through the burbling.

"Home..."

"You'll get there." Tate gripped the back of Wyatt's head. "Just hold on. We'll get you to the sawbones."

"Jacob..."

"None of that!" Tate's eyes burned. "You ain't gonna see Jacob yet!"

"Don't worry..."

Tate tugged Wyatt's hair. "Wyatt Boone, I will tan your hide!"

Wyatt's hand fumbled weakly, and Tate grabbed it. Wyatt's grasp contained a mere ghost of the strength that had pulled Tate from creeks and clapped him on the back a thousand times. His fingers trembled, his skin cooling, and he barely breathed.

"I'll say hi... to—" Wyatt coughed a glob of blood, splattering Tate's ear and cheek. "Sarah... for you..."

A faint breath shuddered out of his mouth. Then, his chest stopped moving. Light abandoned his eyes, leaving behind only blue glass staring dully at an uncaring sky.

Though reluctant to leave Wyatt in the mud for even a single moment, Tate laid him down gingerly, grabbed his Remington, and rose to his feet. Whatever pain he'd felt in his shoulder faded, an echo from someone else's body.

Again and again, Tate fired.

Though he should've taken careful aim—his unit had been low on ammunition for several weeks—he shot at anything that looked blue; as long as that recoil hit his hand and the Remington flashed, he got what he wanted.

Not much point anyhow.

Even as his unit pushed the Yanks back, Tate still lost. His fellow soldiers could cheer all they wanted; Tate could only weep.

Stumbling back to Wyatt's side, Tate reached toward his gaunt face, then gently closed his eyes.

The cries of victory mocked Tate.

How could they cheer when Tate would never hear Wyatt laugh—or even complain—again? All Wyatt had wanted was to return home and hug his ma again.

Tate had promised to get him there; he'd promised the same to Mrs. Boone.

He'd failed. Again.

Just like nine years ago... only this time, he had no excuse.

He couldn't claim he was too young, that he hadn't been there. Wyatt had died right next to him, shielding *him* from Union bullets. Wyatt, whose family had taken him in, the friend who'd filled his life with laughter for nine years, even after he'd lost his own brother.

Gone.

Tate had lost the last remnant of his life before the Comanche attack. He had nothing.

Actually, no, he had one thing—one person.

Lynda.

He'd get home to his wife, even if he had to crawl back to Texas on his hands and knees.

***

Chirping crickets replaced roaring rifles.

Tate had never really thought about one noise replacing another before. Now, however, with the camp back in a semblance of order, he couldn't help but compare. This morning, Wyatt had been telling Tate about the steer he planned to buy once he got back home, and now...

Now, Tate slumped on a fallen log, alone.

Sitting just beyond the ring of firelight, he breathed in the damp Virginia air and winced as the pain in his shoulder flared. The surgeon, a portly man with hands permanently stained the color of rust, had poured whiskey in Tate's wound, stitched it up with horsehair, and wrapped it with faded bandage he'd claimed had been boiled, but which Tate could swear smelled of dead flesh.

Around the fire, men with hollow faces huddled together. Some cleaned rifles. Others—braver men than Tate—stared into the flames.

He didn't dare do the same. Wyatt or older ghosts might come looking for him; yet though the sound had changed, pine smoke and wet earth couldn't disguise the scent of iron and spent powder.

Tate fumbled inside his coat and pulled out Lynda's latest letter. The creased paper, soft as doeskin, had worn thin over the hundreds of times he'd taken it out and folded it back up. This far from the fire, he couldn't really see the neat script and graceful loops, but at this point, her words had branded themselves on the inside of his skull.

My Dearest Tate,

The house is quiet as a tomb without you in it.

After weeks of nothing but dust and baked earth, the Lord finally sent us some rain. The whole prairie smells clean. I wish you were here to smell it with me.

Things ain't right without you. Sometimes, a board will groan, and I'll look up, expecting you to be standing there in the doorway. Your work coat still hangs by the door. When I miss you the most, I bury my face in it. I swear I can still smell you on the collar.

The bed's the worst part. I'll wake in the dead of night, reaching for you, and the empty space beside me feels colder than a banker's heart. I miss listening to you breathe in the dark. I always slept easy, knowing you stood guard over our world.

This ranch is nothing but dirt and wood without you, so don't go chasing glory. Mind yourself, and come back in one piece. That's all the victory I need.

Yours evermore,

Lynda

Tate folded the letter and tucked it back into his breast pocket, placing it over his heart like a poultice.

No other medicine did him any good.

Digging through his rucksack, he found a leather-bound folio, which contained a few sheets of precious paper and a pencil nub, and pulled it out. His shoulder screamed in protest as he balanced the folio on his knee and pressed the nub to the paper.

What do I even write?

Simple words on paper could never convey the burden of the day's events.... yet he had to try; he owed Wyatt that much, at least. His mother deserved to know. The army could take years to get around to informing her. Briefly, he considered giving her those years. To let her think Wyatt still lived.

Shaking his head, he took a deep breath and abandoned the idea, deciding that delaying the inevitable would only make her grief hit harder in the end.

Dearest Lynda,

I pray this letter finds you well. We saw action today. I'm alright. Took a ball in the shoulder, but it's not serious. The surgeon says I'll be fine, so don't worry.

Yet my hand trembles as I write these next lines.

Wyatt fell today. He shielded me after I was hit. He didn't suffer, though. It was quick.

That lie, at least, he could tell. Mrs. Boone didn't need to know how her son had choked on his own blood while the life had drained out of him.

I cannot find the heart to write his ma, my love. I beg you to go to her. Sit with her. Please, don't let her read it in some cold letter from the army. Tell her he was brave, that he was smiling right to the end, happy he'd get to see Jacob again.

I always imagined us riding home side by side, two brothers, arguing about who's the better shot. I cannot picture it now. I wish we were together so I could feel your warmth. The world feels cold without you by my side.

His pencil hovered over the paper.

War, with its speeches, flags, and talk of honor and glory... all smoke—lies old men whispered as they sent boys to die in the muck. Even if the Cause won, Tate and his unit would have nothing to show for it save a field of broken bodies and a list of names to carve into tombstones. Even the Yankees they'd killed today had mothers and wives.

Each soldier traded one heartbreak for another, receiving nothing in return.

Tate closed his eyes for a moment before bending back to his letter.

It is only the thought of you that keeps me breathing, Lynda, knowing you wait for me. Without you, I would have nothing left to live for.

I dream of the day I am reunited with you.

With all my heart,

Tate

Chapter Two

Sherman, Texas, Winter 1865

Four years later

The winter chill seemed to promise a clean slate and a blanket of pure white to cover the soot from which Tate had run. Each snowflake that melted on his face washed away the grime of Virginia mud and the stench of gangrene that'd clung to his memories. The war had ended.

Tate had walked out of hell and made it home.

Four years. Four years of sleeping with one eye open and learning the different whistles Minié balls made as they sought out a man's life. Four years of watching boys who'd never seen a mountain or ocean die, just so a few rich landowners wouldn't have to pay their workers.

Yet he'd survived.

The stagecoach driver had dropped him off five miles back, shaking his head and saying no horse could make it through this blizzard.

Tate didn't mind; the sole on his left boot flapped with every other step, but five miles meant nothing when he'd already crossed a country to get back to his own bed.

To Lynda.

His lips formed her name like a prayer—the only one he had left at this point. Imagining her face and the way her green eyes crinkled at the corners when she laughed, he could almost smell the lavender and woodsmoke that always clung to her hair. He'd read her letters until the ink bled out and the paper turned to felt in his hands.

Cresting the familiar rise, he took his first full breath of air since before he'd left home.

There, as always, the long shape of the house and the sturdy barn crouched amid snowdrifts that had almost risen to Tate's knees. Lynda would have a fire roaring, of course, and stew simmering on the stove. He'd track snow all over her clean floor, she'd curse him for it, and he'd just laugh and pull her into his arms.

The old sentinel oak he'd climbed as a boy, under which he and Lynda had shared a stolen jug of cider on their wedding day, appeared in front of him, then the fence line. The same one Lynda had written about, the one she'd shored up with rocks. Finally, the gate—

What...?

The gate was wrong.

Hanging crookedly on one hinge, it swung in the wind, creaking mournfully, like a grinning drunk showing his broken teeth.

Lynda would never leave the gate like that.

Tate lurched forward, churning through the heavy snow on a path that should've been cleared. Always meticulous, Linda would've been out with the shovel the moment the first flurry had fallen. Yet the snow lay thick and undisturbed.

Then, Tate came upon the house.

No, not a house—a carcass. The front door, which he himself had placed, had been ripped from its frame. Windows had been shattered. The chicken coop had been reduced to a wreck of splintered planks, the snow around it stained with frozen blotches of crimson.

"Lynda!"

Wind and snow swallowing his shout like a hungry whale, Tate broke into a stumbling run. His shoulder screamed in protest as he burst through the ruined doorway and charged past the overturned table, darting between smashed chairs. Lynda's sewing basket lay on its side, spools of thread scattered across the floorboards like colorful tears.

"Lynda!"

Tate scrambled back outside, scanning everything and anything. Slipping and sliding over ice and snow, he sprinted toward the barn as his lungs burned. The sight of the double doors gaping ajar filled his gut with lead, and the mess of kicked-over stalls and scattered hay inside ripped at his throat.

Stumbling back outside into the oppressive whiteout, he turned in a slow circle until the sentinel oak snagged his gaze.

The shape of the tree wasn't right, either; something extra that didn't belong, dark against the mossy bark, dangling from the skeletal branches and swaying in the breeze. Tate's eyes bore into it, but he couldn't comprehend what he saw.

Then, it hit him.

The stench of rot. Cloying sweetness of meat left out too long. Tang of iron that spoke of settled blood.

Interwoven with the ghost of lavender and lye, like clean laundry.

He didn't know why he hadn't noticed it before; it just hadn't *reached* him until now—as if his mind had refused to acknowledge what his senses had told him.

Tate barely breathed as he stepped toward that shape, his boots as heavy as brass cannons. He couldn't understand—didn't want to. His soul begged to escape, to flee back to war, where horrors and death had made sense.

He moved forward, drawn inexorably to the length of rope sagging from that snow-dusted branch, the shape swinging beneath dark threads. To that pair of worn leather boots, the ones she'd worn to muck out the stalls, their soles turned inwards.

He reached the boots, hugged their creased leather... and the cold legs inside them.

It couldn't have happened. Not to Lynda—the bedrock of his entire world—a woman who'd lived and breathed compassion, never saying an unkind word. When Tate had left to go to war, she'd just smiled and told him she'd be here, waiting for him.

He fell to his knees and *screamed.*

As snow soaked through his trousers, the strength that had carried him through Shiloh and Chickamauga, the grit that kept him alive when men all around him were dying, drained from him, vanishing into the frozen earth.

He'd *prayed*; even after what'd happened to his family, he'd prayed. Every single night in that godforsaken war, he'd asked the Lord to keep her safe, thanked Him for giving him something to come home to.

The cold was a *liar*—and so was He.

The uncaring wind howled through the oak's bones, disturbing the rope; the creaking rhythm of the hempen threads burrowed into the crevices of Tate's mind, murky cracks from which his nightmares would draw inspiration. Lynda's simple calico dress fluttered as she were just... dancing.

Such a gentle soul... left for the crows and the cold.

Growling, Tate struck the frozen earth until his knuckles bled. Then, he scrambled to his feet and looked around with stinging eyes, baring his teeth.

Whatever animal had done this, whoever had looked upon Lynda's good nature and rewarded it with a gruesome necktie, must've left a clue behind—*something* Tate could use to track them down, flay them from boot to brow, and salt the wounds.

Bursting back into the ruined house, Tate kicked the overturned table aside and looked for anything that didn't belong, anything unfamiliar. Nothing except a mess of melting snow, mud, and shattered crockery.

Kneeling, he traced the churned-up slurry of wood, water, and dirt on the floor. Whoever had done this either purposefully waited for the snowstorm, or they were the luckiest cuss this side of the Sabine.

Next, he tore through the small bedroom.

The attackers had ripped clothes from chests and drawers and slashed the mattress open.

What could they have possibly been looking for?

Tate and Lynda had had little to steal—a few coins they'd saved in a jar and his mother's silver locket—nothing so valuable that Lynda would've given her life to protect it.

Pressure building behind his burning eyes, Tate kicked and punched the walls, jarring his wounded shoulder, until he slipped and collapsed to the floor with a dull *thump*. Grinding his teeth, he groaned as heat crawled up his joints, as if someone had dragged rusty nails through them.

His energy depleted, he stood up and staggered back outside.

Of *course* he'd found nothing. It had been pointless to even try. That was the story of Tate's life. Everyone he'd ever dared to love died.

He trudged through the swirling snow, wincing at each snowflake that kissed his cheeks.

He had nothing now—no name, face, or direction—only a desecrated grave.

Ma, Pa, Sarah, Wyatt... and now, Lynda.

The last piece of Tate's soul had died.

So he would return to war—only, this time, it would be personal. No matter how long it took, he'd scour the world for the monsters who'd done this. They'd declared the fight against him, and by whatever was left of his blighted soul, he would *finish* it.

But first... Lynda.

Returning to the oak, he looked up the rough bark and clenched his fists. Shooting the rope would only disrespect her memory further. She deserved the effort it would take to climb up there and cut her down.

Holstering his pistol, he pulled himself up, finding purchase in the gnarled trunk. His shoulder screeched with every move, but he gritted his teeth and pushed on. Upon reaching the branch, he shimmied out, pulled his hunting knife from his belt, and sawed at the rope.

The fibers parted with a series of reluctant groans, and the rope snapped.

Scrambling down, he landed hard in the snow moments after her body met the ground with a muffled *thud*. Hands trembling, tears flowing down his cheeks, he crawled to her side.

He couldn't bring himself to look at her face yet.

For now, he gently worked the noose from her neck and threw the accursed rope as far as he could.

Then, he gathered her into his arms.

She was so *cold*. She should've been laughing, vibrating with life, bringing warmth to his days; instead, she slumped in his arms like a sack of grain. Dead weight.

He cradled her against his chest and carried her out of the shadow of that awful tree, her head lolling against his shoulder. After laying her on the porch, he brushed the snow from her hair.

"I'm sorry. I'm so, *so* sorry. You deserved better." He kissed the crown of her head. "You deserved someone who wouldn't have gone away."

A tremor started in his gut, rattling his bones as it clawed up his throat. A jumble of sobbed apologies erupted from his lips, his entire frame convulsing as hot tears flowed into her cold hair. He clung to her, rocking back and forth, as if he could bring her back if he just gave her all the warmth and life he had left.

Eventually, Tate's tears dried up, and he wobbled his way to the barn to retrieve a shovel. Choosing a spot near the porch, where the morning sun would touch first every day, he thrust into the frozen ground.

Thunk

"I'm sorry."

Thunk

"I'm sorry."

Thunk

"I'm sorry."

The first few jabs bounced uselessly off the iron-hard earth, but he kept at it until a small chip of frozen dirt flew up. Not much, but a start.

After that, he fell into a rhythm. *Lift. Plunge. Apologize.* On and on, he dug. It couldn't be a shallow grave.

No matter how long it takes, I'll see to it that—

Suddenly, Tate froze at the sound of a heavy boot pressing into snow.

Crunch.

Instincts honed over years of ambushes and midnight skirmishes screamed at him; he dropped his shovel and drew his Remington. The metallic *click* of the hammer rang like a blacksmith's hammer in the muffled yard.

A man faced him.

"That's far enough, stranger." Tate slowly rose, pointing his pistol at the man, and took a half-step forward. "I'm gonna ask you just once. Your answer decides if you die quick or you die slow.

"You the one who strung her up?"

Chapter Three

Hollister Ranch, Texas, Winter 1867

Two years later

The ranch had become a ghost wearing a dead man's clothes. Tate had rebuilt, plank by bitter plank, but light, laughter, and joy had followed Lynda into the ground.

Now, Tate lived in an empty shell: four walls and a roof, a place to clean his guns and stare into the fire until the flames blurred into a roaring eye.

Amid the smell of boiled coffee, gun oil, and wet wool, Cade Avery hunched over the rough-hewn kitchen table, his lanky frame folded like a carpenter's rule. His hair, the color of sun-cured hay, had grown long and unkempt, and his blue eyes had the same color as the winter sky.

To be fair, none of them cared for vanities anymore.

Opposite Cade, Grady Hawthorne's broad shoulders filled the small space. His beard slouched, a dark thicket streaked with gray, his green eyes brimming with the deep weariness of a man that actually had something to lose. Nursing a tin mug of coffee in his calloused hands, he stared at the map spread between them.

The same night of blood and ruin bound them all together.

Two years ago, after Tate laid Lynda on the porch, he'd aimed his Colt at the man crunching through the snow, ready to send the intruder to hell. However, when the stranger raised his hands, his face had displayed the same shattered horror that churned in Tate's own gut.

Then, through his anguish, Tate had recognized the stranger as Cade Avery, a neighbor he'd only ever nodded to at the general store. The attackers had hit his place, too, robbing him of his wife and two little girls.

Not long after those mangy curs killed his folks and brother, Grady had found them—though, by some miracle, he'd managed to hide his wife and children in the root cellar.

They never spoke of that night; talking would only open a chasm brimming with the faces of the dead. In its place, tracks, leads, and clues filled their quiet. Claims, rumors, and a name that had poisoned the land like a snakebite: the Bone Orchard Boys.

"Reckon tonight's the night." Cade tapped a crudely drawn circle on the map. "Fletcher's word was solid. Them Bone Orchard bastards are holed up yonder in that old trapper's shack north of Whisper Creek."

Grady took a slow sip of coffee and glanced out the snow-lashed window. "Full-blown blizzard brewin'. Gonna be slow ridin' and mean goin', I reckon."

Let the sky fall. Makes no difference.

Two years of chasing whispers and tracking phantoms to a single point on a worn piece of paper.

The trail ends now.

"Snow'll hide our sign and choke the sound." Tate glared at the map. "Ain't a soul alive expects trouble in a storm like this."

Cade nodded. "They'll be half-drunk, bellies warm by the fire, thinkin' the world forgot 'em. We go in quiet—no warning."

Grady scratched his chin. "How many we talkin' again?"

"Fletcher counted eight, give or take."

Grady let out a slow breath. "Three against eight. In a blizzard."

Tate sighed.

It wasn't difficult to guess the reason for Grady's reluctance, and Tate couldn't blame him. Grady's wife and three kids waited for him, praying he'd come back. Tate had nothing. Cade had nothing. Among them, only Grady risked a future, and Tate respected him more than any man on earth for it.

"Grady," Tate began, shaking his head, "best you head on home. Let me and Cade finish this."

"Now, you ain't fool enough to tell me that, Tate."

"This ain't about what's ahead, Grady. It's about squarin' up what's behind."

"You forget what they done to—?"

"Of course not." Tate raised a hand. "I know. But you—"

Grady slammed his palm on the table. "Then quit jawin', Tate! Let's ride."

Tate looked down at his hands. Long ago, they'd belonged to a rancher. Not anymore. Now, his calluses had formed around the grip of a rifle stock and the hammer of a Colt, not the handle of a shovel. His fingers had taken lives instead of setting fence posts. Even now, sporadically, blood seeped from his skin and dripped to the ground.

He looked up at Cade and Grady. "Let's go."

Tate stood and walked to the stone hearth, where his gun belt hung from a peg. The dark leather had gone supple with use. After strapping it on, he checked the action on his Colt with six crisp *clicks*.

Sometimes, this pistol felt more like a part of him than his own skin.

Cade pulled a long-barreled Remington from its holster and spun the cylinder. Grady finished his coffee, set the mug down with a soft *tink*, and went to retrieve his rifle from a corner, where it leaned against the wall beside Tate's.

As he took his Henry rifle from Grady, Tate lost himself in the gleam of metal.

He was ready to die.

Not that he yearned for death—far from it—but he found himself at peace with the idea. After all, his life had ended in this very spot two years ago.

Everything since had led to this moment of reckoning.

After levering a round into Henry's chamber, Tate pulled on his heavy coat, grabbed his hat, and pushed the cabin door open. As a gust of snow charged into the room, tearing at him with icy claws, Tate stepped into the swirling twilight and a maelstrom of white.

***

A man walked differently when hunting other men, and Tate lived that truth with every step he took.

He didn't plod like a rancher checking fence, nor did he march like a soldier to battle; he sauntered like a predator, holding his weight low and stretching his senses taut as new wire.

As the blizzard tried to flay the skin from Tate's bones, his only landmarks were Grady's broad back and Cade's lean silhouette.

The trio spoke in a language of tilted hands and gloved signals, and when they reached the ravine, Tate took the lead.

He led them through timber, trusting his memory more than any map of ink on paper. Snow piling on his shoulders, he navigated by instinct: a subtle shift in the wind that told of a clearing, the faint scent of pine that spoke of denser thickets.

Once, he'd tracked deer in these woods; tracking devils would be no different.

Then, a new scent floated in on a sideways current of wind—so faint, he wondered if his own desperation had conjured it from the frozen air.

Halting mid-stride, he lifted his head. The blizzard offered only snow and resin. Taking another breath, deeper this time, he invited the frigid air in to scour his lungs.

Nothing.

He needed to calm down, be patient, or—

The wind swirled, and the phantom aroma returned with substance: woodsmoke.

It cut through the storm, but not in the way honest smoke from a well-tended hearth would. No, this greasy smog bore the heavy fumes of unseasoned wood burning too fast. Underneath, the cloying odor of cheap fat spitting on a hot skillet snaked along.

Lynda's cooking had never smelled like this; she'd used hickory to cure her bacon and filled the kitchen with the aroma of coffee and baking bread. Now, the snake-bellied bastards who'd killed her even struck at her memory with this stench—parasites, grown fat and comfortable in their den.

Let them feel safe. One more sip of whiskey and one last laugh.

Through a screen of snow-laden branches, his target unfurled: a flicker of orange light, revealing the trapper's cabin. A pinprick of foul life in the heart of a frozen wilderness.

Tate tightened his grip on the cold stock of his rifle until his knuckles cracked.

Two years of his life, every waking moment and every haunted dream, had gone down the drain looking for that little square of light.

At a gesture from Tate, Cade and Grady fanned out in practiced movements, rehearsed a hundred times in the chill shell of Tate's rebuilt barn.

Tate would be the anvil.

Taking the most direct and most dangerous route, he'd head straight to the barn, using the blizzard as a curtain to reach the stack of firewood that ought to be piled near the door. From there, he'd cover the front door and the two main windows.

Grady would be the hammer.

His path angled eastward, where a thick stand of old-growth pines on a slight rise overlooked the cabin. Once settled, he'd have a clear field of fire toward the cabin's eastern face and—crucially—an oblique angle on the front porch.

Cade would be the hidden dagger.

His road swerved west, through the deepest drifts. While Tate drew their eyes and Grady hammered their walls, Cade would slip around and target the back door or the single small window in the rear wall.

As Tate walked, a voice that had, at first, sounded like Lynda's urged him to take as much pleasure from killing her murderers as he could. Yet, the longer it spoke, the sharper it grew, scraping like a file on rusted iron.

That can't be her.

Lynda's floating voice would have whispered of planting seasons and new recipes, never of blood on snow. No, this murmuring belonged to the depths of his own heart.

Suddenly, a muzzle-flash bloomed in the trees to his left, right before a sonorous *boom* assaulted his ears. Another shot answered from the right before the echo had time to die, then another.

Dark shapes burst from the snow-covered shrubbery as riders emerged from the murk like demons.

Tate dropped to one knee and aimed the Henry at one of the silhouettes.

His rifle bucked and thundered with a brilliant flash, and his target fell with a choked cry the wind tore away. Tate worked the lever and exhaled in tandem with the metallic *shuck-shuck* he'd come to trust with his life.

"Cade!" Tate fired again, sending another rider down. "Grady!"

Bullets flying past him, Tate fired, moved, and reloaded. Unfortunately, the blizzard aided his enemy more than him, making ghosts of real men and real men of shadows.

Cade returned fire somewhere ahead before a rider passed between them, and Cade vanished. Grady's massive form skulked behind a thick pine, but the storm swallowed him too.

Tate scrambled, diving behind a granite outcropping that offered some small cover, then wiped icy crust from his eyes and reloaded. Around the edge of the rock, a rider bore down on Tate's position, pistol raised. His bullet nearly took off Tate's ear.

Still, Tate needed only a second to spin out from the other side and bring the rider down.

Slumping back against the rock, Tate dragged drafts of frigid, gunpowder-laden air into his heaving lungs. For a moment, the gunfire stopped, leaving only the endless shriek of wind to scour Tate's ears.

Taking advantage of the lull to push another cartridge into the rifle, he pushed off the rock. He had to find Cade and Grady, and he had little time to—

Suddenly, a familiar force—like a mule's kick—slammed into his left side, throwing him against the granite and knocking air from his lungs. His fingers went numb, and his Henry slipped from his fingers.

A lie...

It had to be a lie; how could a man get shot without hearing the report? Had his blood run so hot that he'd gone deaf? It made a certain grim sense, but he'd never experienced anything like it, despite all the battles he'd been in.

Lynda was alive back then.

Sliding down the rough rockface, Tate folded his legs beneath him.

Wet warmth blossomed beneath his coat; even before he pressed his gloved hand to his side, he knew what he'd find. When he pulled his hand away and looked at it, he sighed and shook his head.

In the swirling gloom, his deerskin glove had gone from tan to glistening crimson.

So much blood...

Chapter Four

Sherman, Texas, Winter 1867

Marietta slid the rag across the bar's scarred surface, collecting rings of condensation from mugs patrons had long since drained, leaving her to deal with the mess. Scrunching her nose at the smell of alcohol and wet wood, she scrubbed at a stubborn stain and grumbled under her breath.

The Walker Saloon should have fallen silent an hour ago; however, a knot of resolute stragglers clung to the tables, their laughter growing louder and uglier as the night wore on.

Outside, a squall shrieked, rattling the windowpanes and slamming snowflakes against the glass. Meanwhile, smoke curled from lamps inside and painted the room in shades of amber and gloom.

It should've been a cozy night, a chance for Marietta to relax by the fire and spend some time with the Good Book. Instead, she was listening to Jedediah Finn bray like a donkey over a losing hand of cards.

"You cheated, you low-down son of a—!"

"I played the hand I was dealt, Jed," Silas Cain slurred, leaning back in his chair. "Ain't my fault you cain't tell a good card from a bad one."

Having grown up around men like these, Marietta knew their type quite well; they came in with the dust of the trail on their boots and a week's pay in their pockets, looking to drown in the bottom of a glass. At first, they talked like decent folk, about such topics as cattle prices and the weather; before long, though, whiskey peeled them back, layer by layer, until only the mean parts showed.

Jedediah slammed his fist on the table. His mug jumped, and what little beer remained sloshed over the sides. "You palmed that ace—I seen it with my own eyes!"

Marietta tightened her grip on the damp cloth. This particular dance, she'd learned by heart: foolish pride that sent chairs flying and fists swinging. *Fool's Ballet*, Robert had called it in letters from the army camp. Men with little to their lives, trying to prove themselves tougher than each other until they all ended up bleeding.

Then, a shadow fell across the room.

Uncle Everett, a mountain of a man whose shoulders strained the seams of his flannel shirt, loomed in the doorway to the kitchen. Filling the opening completely, he stood in the smoky air like a granite statue come to life. A thick walrus mustache, shot through with gray, concealed his mouth as he scanned the room with eyes the color of a stormy sea.

As the piano player, a scrawny fellow named Otis, let his fingers trail off the keys, Jedediah's drunken rage flickered and dimmed under Uncle's heavy gaze.

"Clock on that wall says time decent folk was abed an hour ago."

Jedediah pushed his chair back. "We ain't done, Everett."

"Oh, you're done, alright." Uncle's boots thumped along the floorboards. "Done drinkin' my whiskey, done stinkin' up my place. Collect your friend, and haul your hides home 'fore the storm bites too hard to handle."

Silas pushed himself up, but Jedediah grabbed his arm.

"He owes me!"

Reaching out with a hand the size of a ham, Uncle clamped down on Jedediah's shoulder. Jedediah flinched, his bluster draining from him like air from a punctured bladder.

"He don't owe you nothin'." Uncle's thumb pressed into the juncture of Jedediah's neck and shoulder. "Now, you can walk out on your own two feet, or I can help you find the door with the toe o' my boot. Makes no difference to me."

As men at other tables began to shuffle, pull on coats, and grab hats, Marietta smiled.

Uncle never had to raise his voice; even as the men grumbled, they moved. No one wanted to cross Everett Walker when he got *that* look in his eye.

Uncle let go, and Jedediah stumbled back, rubbing his shoulder. Silas tugged him toward the door, following the rest of the muttering herd of sheep heading out into the cold.

Marietta smiled and shook her head. "I could've handled that, you know?"

After bolting the heavy door behind the last man, Uncle walked up to the bar and collected the dirty mugs himself. "Why should you, when you got me standin' here?"

Marietta plucked a mug from his hand. "I been dealin' with their kind all my life, Uncle. Ain't nothin' new."

"Ain't nothin'?" He stopped and looked her straight in the eye. "Pigs will—"

"Always try an' turn a fair house into a sty." She chuckled and dipped the mug in a bowl of dishwater. "I know."

Snorting, he snatched the rag up and took over wiping the bar.

She looked down at the soapy water. Her entire life had been watching him standing between her and something else.

All too often, his solid frame had caged her in like a wall, messing up some plan of hers or the other. Just last spring, when she'd suggested they invest in a new piano, he'd grumbled about needless expense—and, less than a week later, promptly brought her a new dress.

Other times, like tonight, he took away a burden she *could* carry, but really didn't want to.

As she watched him wipe the bar, for one moment, his mustache lost its gray; his skin smoothed out to the young man who'd stood in the doorway of her small room twenty years ago. His brow had twitched when he'd come to tell her that her parents' carriage wouldn't be coming home.

Then, she blinked, and his age returned.

"Go on up to bed, Etta-girl. I'll finish up down here. Gonna sit a spell by the fire, make sure none o' them fools gets the notion to come back."

Touching his arm through the coarse wool of his shirt, she nodded.

She looked around the empty saloon: the overturned chair, the puddles of beer he would need to mop. It wouldn't have taken her that long to put things to rights, but she'd leave it for him regardless.

It makes him happy to do for me.

Dropping the mug to clatter in the washbasin, Marietta stepped away from the bar and glanced at the door. A bolt and a wooden bar offered a flimsy shield against trouble, but for now, it would have to do. Besides, the chances of anyone bothering them again tonight were low anyway.

As Uncle went to stoke the embers in the great stone fireplace, Marietta dried her hands on her apron. Once or twice, she'd urged him to leave the cleaning for tomorrow, forget about keeping watch, and go to sleep as well, but he always insisted on staying by the fire for a while.

She turned away and had just mounted the stairs leading to her room when a fist struck the thick oak door from the outside, rattling its frame.

Boom. Boom. Boom.

Stopping in her tracks, Marietta exchanged a look with Uncle. No honest traveler knocked like *that*, let alone at this time of night.

Uncle grunted and reached for the sawed-off shotgun under the bar. "Some fool must've forgot his hat."

His voice grated like stones grinding together, but Marietta recognized the set of his jaw. Another drunk, full of whiskey and false courage, had probably decided he wasn't afraid of Everett Walker and had come to try his luck.

Won't they ever learn?

Uncle unlatched the bolt with a loud *thunk* and pulled the door open just a crack. "We're closed—go sleep it off somewhere else!"

A shape emerged from the blizzard, lunging through the doorway, resolving into a man, who crashed onto the floorboards in a heap of snow-caked wool. One hand pressed firmly to his side, he brought the storm with him, a blast of frigid air and swirling flakes that died in the saloon's sudden warmth.

Marietta's breath caught in her throat. Even collapsed on the floor, he was the kind of big man meant for felling trees or breaking sod. Ice encrusted his dark brown hair and messy beard. In the lamplight, his tanned skin had gone pale beneath what looked like grime and blood. A jagged scar sliced through his left eyebrow.

He's injured!

Uncle Everett leveled the shotgun at the man's heaving back. "You got ten seconds to tell me what business you got knockin' down my door 'fore I fill you with buckshot."

Shuddering, the stranger pushed himself up onto one elbow. "Help… me…"

Marietta frowned as she watched his free hand twitch near his pistol. Was this a trick? A ruse to get inside before he and his friends robbed them blind? Then again, he was definitely bleeding—but Marietta wouldn't be surprised if some outlaw gang decided to sacrifice one of their own for a successful ambush.

This land bred men harder than coffin nails, and kindness was often rewarded with a knife in the back.

Then, the man rolled to his side, and lamplight caught his face. She looked upon his dark eyes and found no malice in them. Of course, she still had plenty to learn about reading people, but this man clearly needed help.

You don't turn a blind eye to a man bleeding out on your floorboards.

"Uncle, put the gun down."

Uncle glowered, but lowered the barrel.

Marietta knelt by the stranger. "Where are you hurt?"

He gritted his teeth. "Side… gunshot…"

"Uncle, we need Doc Adams. Can you—"

"No!" The stranger breathed heavily. "No... doctor—please..."

Again, Marietta and Uncle shared a look.

A dying man would refuse a doctor for only one reason: the law—or someone worse—was after him.

Which meant she could tell Uncle to throw him back out into the blizzard with a clear conscience. Let the storm finish the job his enemies had started.

It's the safe thing to do. The smart thing.

However, looking at the blood seeping through his coat, turning the snow around him into pink slush, her resolve wavered.

She exhaled. "Uncle, can you get Nora?"

The stranger shuddered. "Who...?"

"Friend of mine." She frowned. "Knows her way 'round a needle."

The man's head thudded back against the floorboards, but he nodded.

Uncle's gaze shifted from the wounded man to Marietta as he clenched his jaw. For a moment, she feared he'd toss the man out, regardless of what she'd asked. After a long moment, though, he sighed and nodded.

Pulling his coat from its peg and grabbing a lantern, Uncle stepped out into the storm.

With only the shriek of the wind, the soft *thumps* of snowflakes against the windows, and the man's heavy breathing to keep her company, Marietta fetched a clean rag and a bucket of fresh water—she'd have to thank Uncle for thinking ahead and fetching the buckets from the well before the weather had turned—and knelt by the man again.

She dabbed at the grime on his forehead. "Who did this to you?"

He flinched at her touch. "Don't... know..."

More questions burned on her tongue—*Who are you? What kind of trouble have you brought to my door?*—but seeing the sweat beading his brow and the tight clench of his jaw, she held her peace. Even if he could speak, it would be cruel to make him do it right now.

She'd just have to wait.

Seconds stretched into tense minutes before the door burst open again, and Uncle led Nora in, stamping the snow from his boots. Nora's face barely peeked out of her woolen scarf, and she carried a worn leather satchel.

"Get him onto that table," Nora said without preamble, shrugging off her coat, "and bring every candle and lantern you have."

Together, Marietta and her uncle hoisted the stranger onto the nearest table, and his pained cries scraped at the inside of Marietta's ribs. Once they'd put him down, his head fell back against the wood.

Nora took a pair of chipped fabric shears and cut away the man's bloody shirt and coat.

The dark wound at his side pulsed, weeping blood. As Nora pressed a cloth to it and probed gently around the edges, the man's breath hitched. Then, auburn lamplight shining on her prominent cheekbones, Nora looked up at Marietta.

"The ball is still in there, lodged deep. I can clean it and stitch him up, but I can't remove it without the proper tools."

"Meaning what?"

"Meanin', Marietta, this fella needs a doctor. If that lead stays where it is, he won't see the sunrise."

Chapter Five

A ceiling greeted him first; rough-hewn planks, dark with age and smoke, stared down at him from above.

Tate blinked at them through a haze that had nothing to do with smoke and everything to do with the thick fog in his head.

No, not fog. Sludge.

Thick slush filled his skull, fragments of memory swimming in the murk. Splintered events floated up from a dark place, then sank again before he could catch them: a horse, crumpling in a whirl of snow; a gun muzzle, spitting fire; a face, smeared and featureless, looming above him before dissolving.

Lynda.

He'd seen Lynda again. It shouldn't have been possible; Lynda was gone—that, he remembered, at least—yet he'd *seen* her talking to a large man with a walrus mustache. She'd smiled and told him she'd loved him.

No, wait, she couldn't have.

Frowning, he clawed his mind for any solid idea. Name, place, anything. Each thought crumbled the moment he touched it. A rhythm of *bangs* and *clunks* pounded against the bones behind his eyes. The effort crushed him like a boulder, grinding his ribs.

Soft scraping drew his gaze to the side.

A woman sat in a straight-backed chair next to the bed—in which, he realized, *he* was lying—and hunched her shoulders. Head bowed, she worked a needle through a strip of white cloth. Lamplight from a nearby table caught gold threads in a knot of hair at the nape of her neck.

Wait—no...

Lynda's hair had been golden; *this* woman had black hair, which curled down her back, and a jawline like prairie bedrock. Yet her slender fingers danced across the fabric, her petite frame quivering as she hummed. Biting the thread with a sharp tug, she finished her task, set the cloth aside, and looked at him.

Her deep green eyes held the shaded depths of a woodland creek.

"Well, now. Decided to wake up, did you?" A small furrow appeared between her brows. "For a spell there, we thought we'd be measurin' you for a pine box."

Tate tried to speak, but only a dry rasp escaped his throat. He swallowed and tried again, and the effort sent a dull ache through his ribs. "Where...?"

"Walker Saloon. Sherman."

"Who...?"

"You don't remember?" She leaned forward. "You stumbled through our door last night, half-froze and leakin' blood all over my clean floor. Gave us a powerful fright."

Not home?

Actually, it made sense. He'd managed to crawl away from the clearing, but pain and blood loss must've made him delirious. Consequently, he'd mistaken this place for home and this woman for Lynda.

Incredible—to think he'd cling to life desperately enough to crawl through wind and snow when Lynda waited for him on the other side.

Yet, he was still forgetting something, something important...

"Cade—Grady!" He tried to jump up and immediately fell back on the bed.

"Have you gone out of your mind?" The woman lunged toward him and pressed a hand to his good shoulder. "Do that again, and you'll bust every stitch we put in you!"

I have to find them!

Always pushing and hunting, and somehow, he'd messed up the ending. How on God's green earth had those jackals known they were coming? Had Fletcher sold them out? No, no, Fletcher wouldn't do that, but... It made no sense. They'd had the blizzard and darkness for cover, and...

And now, I might've orphaned Grady's kids.

Grady's wife, too, would have lost a husband. Tate... Tate had done to another what those outlaws had done to him.

Oh, Good Lord...

Tate leaned over the side of the bed and threw up.

"Easy, now." The woman pressed a gentle palm to his forehead. "Let it out."

As a branding iron seared his left side, his throat simmered, his vision swimming in a haze of red and gray. Hot pokers twisted in his gut, spreading fire through every nerve in his body. Once he had nothing left in his stomach, his arms gave way, and he collapsed onto the mattress.

"There. You lie down, now."

Tate gasped for air, each new breath a fresh torment that burned his lungs. His forehead grew clammy, and he had to blink back a curtain of sweat and tears.

"Was anyone else with me?"

She shook her head.

"Well, much obliged for patchin' me up."

"Ain't just me you gotta thank. My friend spent half the night pickin' lead out of you with a pair of tweezers because you refused a doctor." She frowned. "My uncle had to hold you down while you thrashed like a wild thing. We poured half a bottle of good whiskey in that hole to keep the rot out. You near bled out on my floor."

He took a deep breath. "Again, much obliged."

She leaned closer. "All that for a wounded stranger who burst in smack-dab in the middle of a blizzard. The least you can do is tell me what in God's name happened out there."

Tate sighed. How could he even explain it? Sure, she'd saved his life, but relating his history with the gang would take all day and night long, time that should be spent looking for Cade and Grady.

He shook his head. "I—"

At that moment, the door creaked open, and another woman entered the room with a steaming bowl that smelled of broth.

She paused in the doorway, radiating a different kind of quiet than that of the dark-haired woman; she had been tense, coiled to spring, but this new arrival seemed relaxed. Strands of hair the color of tarnished pennies escaped her simple braid, framing high cheekbones and a dusting of freckles across the bridge of her nose.

The dark-haired woman smiled. "Look who's up, Nora."

"I can see that."

The dark-haired woman stood and stepped back, then turned back to Tate. "This is the friend I mentioned. She's the one who kept you off a cooling board."

Nora set the bowl on the bedside table and took up the chair by the bed, giving him a look like a man might give a horse with a stone in its hoof. Then, she touched his forehead.

"Fever's broke." She pulled her hand back. "Let's see what we're dealin' with."

Before Tate could protest, she pulled the blanket aside and peeled back the bandage at his side.

He gritted his teeth as a fresh wave of fire spread from the wound. Though she pressed firmly and stitches pulled against his skin, her touch was much gentler than most army doctors Tate had known.

"My stitches're holdin'." Nora applied a clean dressing packed with some pungent herbal mixture. "You're lucky man—one inch to either side, and you wouldn't have a gut left to stitch."

Tate grunted doubtfully, moving his eyes to the ceiling.

Had he been lucky, the Lord would've protected his family fourteen years ago. Lynda wouldn't have seen the business end of a rope. By thunder, if Tate had been *lucky*, he would've had more sense than to cling to life so stubbornly after losing them all.

Nora finished up and washed her hands in a basin. "I brought more than just broth."

The other woman leaned against a dresser and glanced at Tate. "Town buzzin' about somethin'?"

"Sure is." Nora dried her hands on a towel. "Sheriff found a mess up north of Whisper Creek this mornin'."

Tate stared up at the stained planks above him as if his life depended on it.

"Dead horses. Dead men." Nora loomed over Tate, piercing him with a glare. "That where you got that lead, mister?"

Tate's throat lined with sand as he nodded weakly.

"What were you doin' up there?"

"Sheriff's gonna want a word with you."

"You the one doin' the shootin'—"

"We gotta tell him you're here, you know."

"—or just getting shot?"

Their questions buzzed around his head like angry hornets, crowding his muddled thoughts. He owed them some answers—they *had* saved his life, after all—but words lodged in his throat. Already, he'd likely gotten Grady killed; no way in tarnation would he drag more people into his mess.

He turned his head to the wall. "I'm tired."

"I don't give a damn," the dark-haired woman snapped, grabbing his chin and yanking his head back. "You brought gunsmoke and blood to my door. We got a right to know what trouble's followin' you!"

He jerked his chin out of her rough palm and pushed himself up on his good elbow, though the effort sent a white-hot poker through his side. As he glared at her, the faint scent of soap and woodsmoke dredged painful memories from below the murky surface of his mind.

"You ain't got a right to nothin'. Never asked for your help."

"Actually, you *did*, while you were bleedin' out on my floorboards, forcin' us to step over you."

"Then turn me loose and be done with it!"

He didn't have time for this; talking wouldn't help him find Cade or dig Grady out of a snowdrift. He needed to act, not spin yarn while his friends froze in the tinder.

As he swung his legs over the side of the bed, the room whirled and reeled. Weight pressed down on his skull, heavy as an anvil.

Ignore the pain.

Tate had marched through the hell of Chickamauga. Buried Lynda with his own two hands. Dragged himself through miles of dirt and snow. Survived a gunshot wound.

A tiny piece of lead would *not* stop him.

"By all that's holy, what do you think you're doin'?" Nora rushed to his side. "You'll kill yourself!"

"Stay back," he growled.

Planting his feet on the frigid floorboards, he put his hands on the mattress—and *pushed*.

His body screamed, every muscle, sinew, and nerve howling in protest as black spots pierced his vision. The floor dropped out from under him, and his entire frame shook. Yet, he locked his knees, clenched his jaw, and *stood*.

He'd made it to his feet.

Panting now, he rose to his full height. He could walk. Get his rifle and go back out there. Crawl, once again, through the snow—only, this time, for a nobler purpose than his own survival.

Then, his stomach revolted. A spasm seized his gut, and he doubled over, spewing bile and broth he didn't even remember eating onto the floor. His legs buckled.

Arms caught him before he hit the floor. Someone half dragged, half lifted him back onto the bed. As he lay there with the sour tang of vomit still in his mouth, his cheeks burned hotter than any fever.

His body had betrayed him. His own broken flesh held him prisoner.

Fighting to maintain his ragged breaths, he stared at the wall, tracing a crack that resembled a river on some map, and gritted his teeth as cloth swished across the floorboards beneath Nora's hand. The dark-haired woman let out a long breath, and Tate clenched his fist.

He'd never asked for mercy from anyone, never desired pity... yet here he lay.

Helpless.

"When you see the sheriff..." He swallowed, tasting ash on his tongue. "Ask if he found Cade Avery or Grady Hawthorne. He'll recognize their names."

The dark-haired woman placed a gentle hand on his shoulder. "Who should I say is looking for them?"

"Tate—Tate Hollister."

"Pleasure to meet you, Tate." She stepped away from him. "I'm Marietta."

He nodded and closed his eyes.

Look at you, Tate—too damn weak to stand. Putting your friends' fates in the hands of strangers.

He had to accept that he'd done all he could. Yet, as sleep claimed him, bringing dreams of all those he'd lost, Cade and Grady rose out of swirling snow to grab at him with rotting fingers.

Chapter Six

Twitching and mumbling, the stranger slept, his brow furrowed as if he fought a battle behind closed eyelids.

And maybe he does, at that.

As Marietta watched the rise and fall of his chest, Nora finished cleaning the floor.

"Well." Nora threw away the rag and washed her hands. "He's a stubborn cuss, I'll give him that."

Scoffing, Marietta crossed her arms. Stubborn didn't even *begin* to cover it. The man—Tate—had tried to stand with a gut full of stitches after bleeding half his life into the snow. Pride like that could get a man killed.

And the people around him, too.

She didn't owe him a blasted thing; he'd stumbled into her world, a complication she neither needed nor wanted, yet...

He'd asked for help—not for himself, but for his friends. She could help with that, at least.

Cade Avery. Grady Hawthorne.

"Reckon he'll be alright on his own for a bit?" Marietta looked at Nora. "We ought to visit the sheriff. Ask about those names he mentioned."

Nora nodded, packing salves and bandages back into her leather satchel. "Maybe we can find out what kind of hornet's nest Tate Hollister kicked over."

Before long, they stepped outside to find the world changed.

The blizzard had howled itself into exhaustion, leaving behind a thick blanket of impossibly white snow, softening every hard edge of town. Glittering fluff clung to the eaves of the saloon, mounded on the porch railing, and transformed the muddy street into a pristine path. Morning sunlight struck the fresh powder, making the whole scene sparkle.

Pine wreaths, dusted with snow and tied with faded red ribbons, hung on the doors of the mercantile and the blacksmith's shop. Garlands of holly drooped from wooden awnings. Sharply scented woodsmoke curled from every chimney, promising warmth and coffee within.

With Christmas rapidly approaching, Sherman wore the season like a new coat.

To Marietta, however, the festive peace tasted like a lie—a pretty bandage over a festering wound. How could the world look so clean when men lay dead in the woods, and a gunshot victim slept in her upstairs room?

As she and Nora ambled down the street and the chill bit her cheeks, Marietta pulled her shawl tighter. That poor man had walked through this last night while bleeding—no, worse: the blizzard had still raged then.

Stubborn, indeed.

They dropped by Miller's Mercantile first.

As they stepped inside, heat hit them in a welcome wave; the air purred with the smells of coffee beans, cured leather, and drying wool. A small crowd of grim-faced townsfolk gathered near the potbelly stove, murmuring among themselves.

Old Man Miller stopped weighing a sack of flour and looked up at them, squinting through the spectacles perched on the end of his nose.

"Mornin', Marietta, Nora." He went back to what he'd been doing. "You here for supplies or gossip? I'm flush with both today."

Marietta exchanged a glance with Nora.

"Sheriff found 'em, I hear." Pike, a cattleman with a scar crossing his left cheek, shook his head. "Word is, it was them Bone Orchard Boys."

"Hogwash," a man with a bulbous nose argued. "Ain't no one fool enough to tangle with that bunch."

A shiver traced a line down Marietta's spine. She knew the name; everyone did.

The Bone Orchard Boys had been plaguing ranches south of the river for years. They'd hit hard, then vanish, leaving behind nothing but bodies, ropes, and stories to keep children awake at night.

"Well, someone did." Pike spat some tobacco. "Sheriff's man said they found three sets of tracks leadin' to that cabin."

"No one got that much sand in 'em, Pike." The other man snorted. "Stop spinnin' yarns."

Marietta crossed her arms. "Sheriff say who they were?"

Pike shrugged. "Just that they was ranchers, by the look of the gear they left behind."

Old Man Miller laughed. "For once, I know more than you, Pike! You owe me a drink."

Pike laughed back. "Bet's a bet. What you heard?"

"Word is, two of 'em made it out. One of them hunters went with Sheriff Sharpe, followed their tracks back to Avery's spread."

Marietta dragged Nora out before anyone could think to ask any uncomfortable questions. Still, she now understood the man in her saloon better than before.

If Tate and his friends really *had* attacked the Bone Orchard Boys—chances were fifty-fifty with how easily folk in this town trusted rumors—it made sense that he wouldn't want to talk about it.

After Miller's, their path led straight to the sheriff's office, a sober thing of plain plank walls at the end of the street. Unlike all the others, this building had no festive wreath on it. Even the smoke trickling from its chimney smelled foul.

As they approached, raised voices seeped through the door.

"...doin' all I can, I tell you!"

"Doin' *nothin'* is what you're doin', Sharpe!"

After a moment of hesitation, Marietta pushed the door open.

The odors of stale coffee and oiled steel met her, mingling with the damp chill of a fire fighting a losing battle. Sheriff Sharpe, a tall man with a politician's smooth face and eyes that never quite settled, sat behind a large desk cluttered with papers. A silver star sat on his chest, polished to a high gleam.

Two men faced the sheriff, mud and snow caking their torn clothes. One, tall and lean, paced around Sharpe's desk like a caged tiger; the other, broad and solid, stood in front of Sharpe like a statue.

"My boys are out there now." The sheriff raised his hands. "We'll pick up the trail again once this weather settles some."

The lanky one whirled around. "The trail's *cold* now! You should have gone out last night!"

"In that blizzard?" The sheriff chuckled. "We do things by the book here, Cade. I won't risk losin' good men on a slim chance Tate made it out of that all-fired mess alive."

Marietta stepped forward. "Tate?"

All three men turned.

The sheriff straightened his brocade vest. "Marietta. How can I help you?"

She looked at the two ranchers. "The man you were with—what does he look like?"

The lanky one took a step toward her. "Big man, built solid. Dark hair, dark eyes."

Marietta smiled. "You two best come with me."

***

The men followed her out of the sheriff's office.

Their boots crunched over the fresh snow with the heavy tread of men who carried heavier burdens than winter coats, scanning the street as though expecting trouble to leap from behind every snow-draped barrel.

Which, if they really *had* tussled with the Bone Orchard Boys, might actually happen.

As they walked, Marietta kept her eyes ahead, fixed on the swinging sign of her saloon. Not like she had much to say to men like these. After the night they'd had, small talk would be an insult. Words of comfort would just ring hollow.

No, it was best—and easiest—to keep her eyes forward and move along.

Inside the saloon, the scent of Nora's salve and the faint tang of blood lingered in the air. Uncle Everett looked up from polishing the bar and narrowed his eyes at the two strangers.

Marietta nodded toward the stairs. "He's up there."

They rushed up, and she walked up to Uncle, hoping to put him at ease with her smile.

"Don't worry. They're friendly."

He sighed. "Better be careful, Etta-girl. Playin' the good Samaritan can get you buried."

"Don't worry." She rubbed his shoulder. "He'll be healed up and gone in a few days. Things will get back to how they were."

With that, she followed them up, escorted by Uncle's grumbles. She reached the room, but hovered in the doorway, feeling like an intruder in a story that had begun long before she'd had any part in it.

The lanky one crouched by the bed. "Tate! By God, you're alive!"

Tate pushed himself up on his elbow. "Cade... Grady. I've never been so glad to see two ugly faces in my life."

The broad one, who must be Grady, let out a shuddering breath. "We looked for you, but the storm swallowed your tracks."

Who are these men?

Marietta had seen friends celebrate with back-slapping and whiskey, seen them mourn with fists and curses. Never before had she witnessed a reunion like this, which spoke of shared battles, common losses, and a bond forged in a crucible she could only guess at.

Tate coughed. "The gang?"

"Scattered." Cade stood up from his crouch. "We put a few of 'em in the ground, but not enough. The rest vanished into the storm like ghosts."

Grady rubbed his chin. "I don't want to say it, but Fletcher might've sold us out."

Tate shook his head. "He'd never—"

"The sheriff's man found his body at the cabin. Shot in the back."

Tate's jaw tightened.

"Tate... There's more." Cade looked away. "We rode to your place from mine, hopin' you'd made it back."

Marietta stepped forward. Oh, this wouldn't be good. When someone took this long to get to the point, it usually meant they had bad news. Likely, someone had robbed Tate blind, or someone he knew had died. Hopefully, it would be the former; the poor man had dragged his bleeding body through a blizzard—she hated to think he'd lost someone too.

Tate frowned. "Spit it out, Cade."

"They torched your ranch, Tate." Grady stared at the floor. "The house, the barn—everything. It's all gone."

Tate closed his eyes and clenched his hand into a white-knuckled fist.

Somehow, this news felt like a mixture of both options Marietta had considered. Still, Grady hadn't mentioned anything burning other than buildings. Hopefully, that meant no one had died in the fire.

Still, he'd lost his spread, and Marrietta felt for him. He'd have to impose on one of his friends, who likely had families, since they hadn't invited him to stay with them already. Having seen his reaction when she'd tried to help earlier, she was *not* looking forward to hearing that conversation.

Unless...

"You can stay here."

The three men gaped at her as one.

"This room's empty most times." She looked directly into Tate's eyes. "You can stay while you heal up."

"I appreciate the kindness, ma'am," Tate replied, shaking his head, "but I won't be a burden on you."

He had the look of a wolf caught in a trap, wary of the hand that offered assistance, and she could guess why. Whoever Fletcher had been—whether friend or trusted informant—he'd betrayed them; for her part, Marietta was little more than a stranger, with no way to guarantee that she wouldn't sell him out for some coin.

It's exactly the sort of thing Uncle would warn me to be careful about.

"It ain't kindness—it's for my own selfish peace of mind." She walked up to the bed. "Those were *my* floorboards you bled all over, and if you leave before recovering from that wound of yours, I won't have a moment of sleep for nightmares of you dyin' halfway to your spread."

A ghost of a smile touched his lips. "I'll manage."

"I don't care." She clenched her jaw. "You're stayin' here, and—"

Suddenly, a *crash* interrupted her—the sharp shatter of glass downstairs, the heavy *thud* of wood hitting the saloon floor, and a bellowing roar.

Marietta's head snapped to the door.

Uncle!

Chapter Seven

Long ago, Tate had become familiar with the sound of things breaking.

The sharp crack of a dry branch underfoot that signaled a spooked deer. The splintering groan of a fence post giving way to a panicked steer. The wet thump of bone yielding to a Minié ball.

Oh, Tate knew them all *too* well.

Of them all, the noise from downstairs—which spoke of wood breaking and glass shattering—was his least favorite: someone was shooting *inside* the saloon.

Gunshots rattled the spoon in the bowl of broth on the nightstand and vibrated his bones through the thin mattress, echoes from six years ago, when it'd stolen the light from Wyatt's eyes.

Not again.

Even as his side burned, he gritted his teeth and pushed himself up. No way would he lie here like a useless sack of meat while Marietta fought a battle *he'd* brought to her door. Especially after she took him in like a stray dog and saved his life.

His own spread lay in ashes. His friends had nearly died in an ambush he'd led them into. Everything he touched turned to ruin.

Not here.

They wouldn't torch this place. After failing Pa, Ma, Sarah, Wyatt, and Lynda, Tate refused to let anyone else die because of him.

A deep growl rumbled in his chest as he swung his legs over the side of the bed.

The room tilted like a ship in a storm. Black spots swarmed his vision like flies on a corpse. Sweat poured down his face. Every muscle in his body howled. The stitches strained as his flesh attempted to tear itself open again.

Yet, no matter how much he struggled, his legs could no more hold him than a length of wet rope could.

Fine. I don't have to walk.

Sliding from the bed, he hit the floor with a heavy *whump*, jarring every bone within him. He sucked in a sharp breath through his teeth. For a long moment, he lay there, floorboards pressing into his cheek against as he breathed in dust and the scent of old pine.

Downstairs, the cacophony continued.

He rolled to his good side and pushed himself up onto his elbow. Bile rose in his throat, but he forced it back down. He looked around the small room, searching in vain for his gun belt, Colt, and Henry. Of course they wouldn't be here; these people had saved him, but he had yet to earn their trust.

Smart play, leaving me weak and weaponless.

And so, he crawled.

His arm and legs did the work, dragging his left side like a dead weight. Each hitching pull across the floor scraped his torn shirt against his wound. A damp smear of pink on the wood trailed behind him. He barely noticed when a splinter dug into his hand.

Finally, he made it to the door.

Now, I just gotta open it.

As he hauled himself halfway up the frame, his breaths clawed their way out of his lungs; he had to pause and lean against the wall to stop his head from spinning. Several shallow gasps later, he wrenched the door open.

A scream rushed upstairs to greet him.

Tate lurched into the narrow hallway. The top of the stairs lay ten feet away—ten feet of open country with no cover. Sliding along the wall, he dragged his shoulder across the rough planks. The sharp smell of gunpowder drifted up the stairwell, mixed with the stench of spilled whiskey and... blood.

He reached the top of the stairs and looked down.

That's one steep flight.

A man could break his neck falling down a set like this, and Tate was barely upright. No, humiliating as it was, he'd have to swallow his pride and slide down.

Gritting his teeth, he sat on the top step, resting on his good hip, and pushed off.

He slid down on his side, bumping and jarring with each step. Every nerve screamed. His vision grayed at the edges. The taste of blood filled his mouth. But many, *many* bumps and bruises later, he landed in a heap at the bottom.

Ain't never doin' that again.

He'd been lucky to land with his spine intact. His side throbbed and burned, his wound gaping open as the stitches gave way. Still, he'd made it downstairs.

Now, he only had to figure out *how* he was going to help.

No gun, barely mobile, Tate doubted he could even cause a doggone distraction. He'd be pumped full of lead before he managed to say his final prayer. But if it was *them*, if the Bone

Orchard Boys had attacked, he'd sink his teeth into their ankles if he had to.

The main room of the saloon swam into focus, a vision from a soldier's nightmare.

Tables lay overturned. Chairs sat shattered into pieces. Broken glass littered the floor, catching lamplight like chips of dirty ice. Two men in heavy winter coats lay sprawled on the floor, their bodies twisted at odd angles. A dark stain spread across one of their chests; the other lay facedown in a pool of whiskey and blood.

Tate's heart skipped a beat as he recognized them; on one of his rare trips downstairs, he'd seen them in the main room, alternatively cursing and smirking over hands of poker.

Victims...? Or were they in on this?

Near the bar, Cade swung a chair leg like a club, keeping a man with a long knife at bay. Grady stood over another attacker, a bloody poker clutched in his big fist.

Then, he saw Marietta.

She stood behind the bar and clutched a sawed-off shotgun with white knuckles. Though her face had gone pale, she glared at a tall man with a face like a starved wolf as he moved toward the end of the bar.

Tate's blood ran cold. He knew men like that, who enjoyed fear, who fed on it.

I have to do something!

Marietta kept the twin barrels level with the man's chest—a clean shot; all she had to do was squeeze the trigger, and that would be it. But her arms trembled as her eyes darted toward Cade, who had his own problems.

She's never killed a man, Tate realized.

Why would she have? Likely, the most violent act she'd performed had been throwing out rowdy guests late at night. She wouldn't have seen trenches, blood-soaked mud, or Minié balls flying through skulls.

Do something!

But he couldn't. If he called out to her, he'd be in a pine box before he could blink. The fact that no one had seen him thus far was a miracle in and of itself. He could only crawl forward and try to grab the man's leg, or something of that nature, to distract him.

So he crawled.

"Put the gun down, little lady." The man ambled toward her. "I'll make it quick for you."

Marietta's jaw tightened, and she took a step back, hitting the wall of bottles behind the bar. Then, she grabbed a half-full bottle by the neck and flung it. The bottle spun end over end in a streak of dark glass and amber liquid.

The wolfish man raised an arm, and the bottle shattered against his forearm with a sound like a gunshot. Glass and whiskey sprayed across his face. He howled, stumbling back and wiping his eyes with his sleeve.

The strike distracted Cade's opponent, too, just enough for Cade to bring the makeshift club down hard on his wrist. A wet *crack* echoed in the saloon. The man screamed and dropped his knife. Cade swung again, a solid thump to the side of the head, and his opponent crumpled.

At the same time, two men, who had circled Grady, looked from their downed friends to Marietta's shotgun, now aimed squarely at the wolfish man's gut. They exchanged a look and bolted for the door.

Marietta gripped the weapon and shook violently.

"Stop!" Tate rasped. "Let him go."

"Tate?" Cade gaped at him. "What in tarnation are you doin' down here?"

Marietta's eyes never left the wolf-faced man.

Tate hardly wanted to let a member of the thrice damned Bone Orchard Boys live, let alone leave, but he couldn't let a good woman like her—who'd saved a stranger's life, offering him room and board while expecting nothing in return—execute a man in cold blood.

"Cade." She gulped. "Can you—"

"Let him go." Tate dragged himself closer. "Ain't no difference if your finger pulls the trigger or you ask another's to. It's a stain you'll carry."

"The sheriff—I… I ought to get the sh—"

"Let him *go*," Tate groaned as his side burned, "and *I'll* take him down myself once I'm healed."

She sighed and lowered her shotgun.

The wolfish man bolted out of there like the wind.

Cade and Grady panted and leaned against the walls, and the fire in the hearth crackled softly. The mingled smells of gun smoke, spilled liquor, and fresh blood hung in the air, a foul stew Tate was growing far too well-acquainted with.

From beneath an overturned table, Nora crawled out. Sawdust and dirt smudged her cheek. Nearly slipping on a jumble of cards strewn across the floor—remnants of an abandoned poker game—she pushed herself to her feet and rushed to Cade, who nursed a bloody knuckle.

Marietta slowly scanned the wreckage of the saloon until her gaze came to rest on something behind the bar that Tate couldn't see from his position on the floor.

"Uncle?"

She vanished from Tate's view, then made *the sound*.

Others might've called it a scream, but this sound started deeper, in a place far beyond words. The ragged howl tore from her throat, clawing its way out of her gut.

Tate himself had made it before—twice: kneeling in the snow two years ago, clinging to Lynda's cold body, and before that, when soldiers had dragged him from his family's cabin and Sarah's little corpse.

It was the sound of the world ripping your still-beating heart out of your chest and showing it to you—before crushing it in its fist.

Just a bit farther...

He pushed himself up onto his elbow and made his way to the bar. As she came into view, he found her on her knees beside the body of a man with a walrus mustache. Tears streamed down her face, and she shook her head as she rocked back and forth on the balls of her feet.

"Please wake up. Please, Uncle, *please*—just wake up!"

Tate reached her and tried to rise to hug her properly, but his legs had no more stability than a hangman's rope.

So he did the only thing he could: lying there, on the floor, he hugged her legs, pressing his forehead against her thigh.

Hopefully, she'd forgive the breach of etiquette under the circumstances, because he wasn't letting go. She needed the same comfort Cade had given Tate two years ago.

Sobbing, she pressed her forehead to the crown of his head and put her hands on his temples. Her tears soaked his hair, and she screamed into his skull.

"Why'd you stop me? I should've sent that devil to hell!"

"Yes." He tightened his hold. "But not like that. Not the first one."

"I'll kill them." She clenched her fingers in his hair. "I'll kill every last one of them, I swear it on the grave. I'll see their blood on the snow if it's the last thing I do."

Tate breathed in slowly.

In his mind, he could see the road unfurling before her: the same cold patch of empty dirt he'd walked for two years. A path that held only iron for food, gunpowder for drink, a grave for your enemies—and, if you weren't careful, another for yourself.

"I know you will. I'll be right there with you."

Chapter Eight

Three weeks.

Three weeks since Marietta and Nora had scrubbed Uncle's blood from the floorboards with lye and stiff-bristled brushes. Three weeks since the good people of Sherman had stood on a wind-whipped hill and bowed their heads as a preacher spoke hollow words over a fresh pine box. The dirt they'd thrown on the lid had clattered like dry bones.

That rattle still followed her into sleep.

The saloon just didn't seem to hold heat like it used to. Chill drafts crept upward from gaps in the floorboards constantly.

Or, maybe, it was just her heart that had gone cold.

Marietta dragged a damp rag across the bar. She'd filled the bullet hole in the wall behind her with putty, but her eyes found it anyway: A small, dark star in the polished wood. Another marred one leg of the piano.

Scars. The whole saloon bore scars now.

Just like me.

Uncle's chair sat empty at the corner table. He should be slouching there, a mug of coffee steaming in his big hand, his mustache hiding a small smile as he watched her work. He'd clear his throat and rumble, *"Etta-girl, you'll wear the wood down to nothing with all that polishing."*

He'd never sit there again.

A fist squeezed her lungs as she gripped the edge of the bar, her knuckles white against the dark wood, and huffed.

A heavy beat thumped on the ceiling above, then the scrape of wood on wood. A minute later, Tate and Nora appeared at the top of the stairs. She'd wedged her shoulder under his arm, taking most of his weight. In his other hand, he gripped the handle of a shovel, using it like a cane.

He moved like a man made of glass.

Each step sent a tight shudder through his frame, and the muscles in his jaw bunched into hard knots. Sweat beaded his temples, but his dark eyes fixed on the table where Cade and Grady waited for him.

Marietta's chest throbbed.

For three weeks, she'd climbed those stairs with bowls of broth or fresh bandages. He'd spoken little—she'd done most of the talking—but he'd listened, a mess of stitches and bruised flesh propped against the headboard, and let her gab.

Shaking off her reverie, Marietta rushed to help get him down the last few steps. A faint smell of herbs and clean sweat clung to him. They settled him into a chair, then took their own seats.

With everyone so grim, the scene resembled a war council.

Cade drummed his fingers on the table, stopped, and started again. Grady rested his big hands on his knees, blocking the window with his broad shoulders. Nora's eyes darted around, making Marietta think of a stray kitten who'd fallen into a pit of dogs.

Between them, a worn map lay spread on the table. Crudely drawn circles and lines crisscrossed its surface like spiderwebs. The heart of the web—a dark cross north of Whisper Creek—marked the place where everything had gone wrong.

Where Uncle's fate had been decided.

Over the last few weeks, she'd found herself blaming Tate for Uncle. She couldn't help it. If he just hadn't come into their saloon, Uncle would be here right now. However, as Tate hadn't told her *why* he attacked the gang—only that they'd wronged him as they'd wronged her—she realized how wrong her view of the situation had been.

After all, she'd sworn to do the same thing he had.

He hadn't come to them intending for those men to kill Uncle. Any dying man—and he *had* been dying—would've looked for help, and a saloon seemed a more sensible choice than someone's house.

Grimacing, Tate leaned forward. "Three weeks is long enough. Those vipers won't lick their wounds forever."

Cade tapped his finger against the table. "Then we oughtta go huntin'."

Grady shook his head, brushing the front of his woolen shirt with his beard. "We oughtta find help, is what we oughtta do."

Tate snorted. "Like we found Fletcher?"

"That ain't fair, Tate." Grady looked away. "They could've beaten it out of him."

"Doesn't matter how they knew." Cade shrugged, then muttered, "Can't trust a soul in this town."

"Cade and I will pick up the trail." Tate pinned his gaze on the map. "We move quiet. We move alone."

Alone.

The word sounded right. Safe. After what had happened here, in her own saloon, where men she'd seen in town a dozen times attacked her, trust would be a fool's luxury.

Every face on the street looked different now.

Old Man Miller, weighing flour at the mercantile. The aptly named Smith, working his glowing forge. Even Sheriff Sharpe, who represented the *law*, with his politician's smile. Any one of them could hide a devil. Any could have sent those men crashing through her door.

"That's a fool's plan, Tate, and you know it." Grady set his jaw. "We rode into eight guns! We were lucky to get out with our hides. We don't know who's pullin' the strings or how many *more* guns he's got."

"Can't surprise them no more." Cade leaned over the table. "Two men make less noise than five. We can live off the land. Go to ground."

"And what about my wife and girls? While you two are out chasin' ghosts in the snow, they're supposed to live under the shadow of these animals?"

"One loose tongue, Grady, and they bring the whole pack down on us." Tate smashed his fist against the table. "They killed Marietta's uncle, Grady!"

"He's right." Marietta pressed her lips into a line. "My uncle served drinks in this saloon for twenty years. Some of those men we put in the ground drank and played cards right at this table. We can't trust *anyone*."

Nora gulped. "Marietta, that's wild talk."

Marietta breathed in air tasting of blood and smoke. "The leader of the Bone Orchard Boys could be anyone, Nora. He could be the storekeeper. He could be the farrier."

The ticking of the grandfather clock in the corner sounded like a hammer striking an anvil. Grady's face hardened. Cade inclined his head at her.

Tate held her gaze the longest.

She didn't need a nod or a word of agreement; the look that passed between them told her all she needed to know. He understood; suspicion seeped into your skin, twisting the world until a neighbor's friendly wave looked like a threat—yet Marietta felt that Tate, at least, was worthy of her trust.

Grady planted his hands on the table, making the wood groan. He looked like a bear on its hind legs, a wall of flesh between Tate and the door.

"This can wait. You look like death warmed over, Tate! You need another week—at least."

Nora put a hand on Tate's shoulder. "I patched you up twice, Tate. The third time might not take."

Tate's jaw worked, but Nora's words had broken the storm gathering in his expression. Looking from Grady to Nora, then finally dropping his gaze to the floor, he nodded.

Cade let out a breath, grabbed his hat, and jammed it on his head. "Fine. A week. But I'm going to spend it watching the sheriff. He didn't look for Tate, and no matter what he says, it smells worse than a week-old fish."

Grady nodded. "You do that. I'll see to my family and put the word out, careful-like. See who might stand with us when the time comes."

They filed out one by one.

With just Marietta and Tate left, the room echoed like a cavern. The fire crackled and spat in the hearth as Marietta picked up the tin mugs and stacked them with a series of metallic *clinks*. That done, she folded the map and tucked it on a shelf behind the bar.

Work—that's the thing.

She needed to fill her hands and stop them from shaking.

Taking a rag, she wiped down the already clean bar. *Back and forth.* The repetitive motion soothed the frantic flutter in her chest. *Back and forth.*

"Nora tells me the townsfolk been waggin' their tongues."

Marietta's hand stilled. "Folks always talk."

"About the saloon. About business."

Her spine stiffened.

Over the past three weeks, a mere handful of customers had shuffled in, avoiding her eyes, hastily consumed a single drink, and tossed a few coins on the bar before scurrying out. Whispers on the street had stopped the moment she approached. Old Man Miller suddenly found something important to count on a high shelf whenever she entered the mercantile.

They treated her saloon like a plague sign had been nailed to the door.

She thought of the dwindling sacks of flour in the pantry, the low level of whiskey in the good barrel, and the ledger under the bar, whose negative numbers grew long and greedy, while the positive ones dwindled shyly.

"We'll get by." She shrugged. "Folks are spooked. It'll pick up."

The fire popped as a log collapsed amid a shower of embers.

Tate pushed himself up from the chair with a grunt, steadying himself with the makeshift cane. Moving slowly, he came around the table, then stopped at the bar.

How can a man look so frail, yet so solid at the same time?

"You've given me a roof. A bed. Nora's mendin'." He jerked his chin toward the empty room. "Reckon it's time I earn my keep."

She clutched the damp rag. "What're you gettin' at?"

"I can work. Never poured a whiskey in my life, but I can haul barrels. Stack wood. Stand the door, make sure folks mind their manners." He shifted his weight with a grimace. "I pick things up quick."

Her first instinct was to refuse.

I don't need your help. I don't need your pity. I am Marietta Walker—this is my place, and I can handle it.

It sounded like something Uncle Everett would've said—but Uncle's stubborn pride had followed him into the cold ground.

She looked around the empty room. Chairs sat vacant. The piano stood silent. Wreaths already hung over the doors, and Uncle had draped a garland of pine boughs behind the bar before she'd lost him.

As things stood, come Christmas Eve, she'd be celebrating all alone among the decorations.

Instead of Uncle mulling cider on the stove and lighting lamps, her only company would be the wind and rattling windows.

Maybe it'd do me some good to have some help around here.

"The wood box needs filling," she whispered, "and the cellar steps are slick. I nearly broke my neck last week."

He held her gaze.

Then, the rarest thing happened: the hard lines of his face softened as the corners of his mouth lifted, pulling his rough beard, and stretched into a sliver of a smile that crinkled the corners of his eyes.

Warmth spreading through her fingers, Marietta's own lips twitched to answer his smile without asking permission, and a blush crept up her neck.

Then, a scream ripped through the windows from the outside.

Chapter Nine

Tate watched Marietta duck behind the bar and rise with a Winchester in her hands. Working the lever with a metallic *shuck-shuck*, she shoved it into his chest.

"Go."

He nodded and made for the door. His speed still left a lot to be desired, but he didn't have to crawl this time, at least. Pushing through the batwing doors and onto the porch, he shielded his eyes as white slammed into him.

Tate squinted. *Of course.*

It just *had* to be snowing. Again. What in God's name had possessed the sky this year? He'd seen more snow in the last month than in the previous two years combined—not to mention how the blasted stuff fell in thick curtains, blurring the edges of the street and muffling sound.

Dark shapes scrambled for doorways and awnings. A riderless horse galloped past. At the far end of the street, two or three riders were already fading into the storm like phantoms, leaning low over their saddles.

Are those the—?

Before he could finish the thought, they vanished; Tate hadn't even had time to draw a proper bead.

Planting his feet on the snow-dusted porch, he swept the rifle barrel over the street. The failed ambush of the cabin had taught him a hard lesson: look only at the visible threat, and the one you don't see will kill you. But no muzzle flashes bloomed from the rooftops. No second wave of riders charged down the street.

Then, Tate's stomach clenched as a coppery smell hit him, and he ambled down the porch steps.

The street looked like a butcher's yard. Two steers lay dead in front of the smithy, throats cut and legs tangled. Another rested on its side in front of Miller's Mercantile, its belly slashed open to spill its guts onto the ground in a coiled mass of pink and gray.

The buzzards hadn't come just to wake snakes; no, they'd butchered cattle and left the poor beasts to rot in the middle of the main street. Someone wanted to leave a message, a warning in blood and intestines, for the whole town to read: *We own this place. We can touch you whenever we want. We can bleed you dry.*

Apparently, the Bone Orchard Boys hadn't just been boiling coffee over the last few weeks.

Granted, with business so slow, they hadn't heard much news lately—not to mention that Tate had been focused on rest and recovery, Marietta had been consumed with grief for her uncle—so Tate wasn't sure if any more ranches had been hit. In any case, this attack made sense as a general scare tactic.

But why bother scaring the people of Sherman?

No one here had that much money. Not right now, anyway. Sure, the place was growing quickly and promised to develop into a significant town in the future, but right now, there were so many better places for the gang to bother—which meant something more than money was at play here.

Whoever led the Bone Orchard Boys had some other purpose with Sherman; Tate just couldn't figure out what it was. It wasn't that important right now anyway. The gang would still be here tomorrow.

Today, Nate had people to help.

Smith stood frozen in the doorway of his smithy, a hammer dangling limply from his hand, looking pale as the ashes beneath his forge. Old Man Miller peeked out from behind his doors. Many others peered from behind closed curtains.

The scene reminded Tate of Shiloh; after the first volley had hit, half the boys who'd been singing an hour before had screamed and damn near broke, but a good half managed to brace themselves for the incoming fight.

You either choked or you shook it off and got to work.

Lowering his Winchester, Tate approached the mercantile. "Miller! You got a winch on that wagon of yours?"

Miller's head barely made it past the door. "They gone?"

"Long gone." Tate took a limping step toward him. "Fetch some rope—we gotta drag these beasts off the street before they freeze to the ground!"

That broke the spell.

Smith looked from Tate to the dead steer, then at his own hands, as if only now remembering what they were for. Dropping the hammer with a clatter, he disappeared into his shop. Miller blinked and nodded, then vanished inside like a skittering bird.

Tate walked up to the nearest steer. The blood had already started to congeal, turning a darker shade of red. The glassy black orb of the beast's eye stared up, unseeing, at the falling snow. Tate had seen that same empty look in the eyes of too many men.

His side protested as he reached down, grabbed one of the steer's horns, and pressed his palm to its side.

Grunting, he pulled, trying to shift to immense weight, even if only by an inch.

Miller returned with a length of thick rope, trailed by the blacksmith. "Here."

"Hitch 'em by the horns." Turning to Smith, Tate said, "We'll use your anvil for purchase."

The man looked at him, then at the dead animal. "What's the use? Them coyotes'll just be back."

"Reckon they will." Tate's breath misted in the air. "And when they come, we can either be kneelin' in a street full of rot or on our feet, ready to fight. Now, get to it."

The smith nodded, and they got started. While Miller looped rope around the steer's horns, Smith strode quickly into his shop. A loud grunt later, he emerged with his anvil.

As they worked, other men crept hesitantly into the street with pale faces and wide eyes. They looked at the carnage, then at Tate, as if waiting for direction.

Poor folks must've forgotten how to stand together.

Tate resolved to remind them.

Moving from man to man, he spoke in a low, steady voice, like a rancher facing a tough job. Simple. Direct. Practical. *Get a shovel. Clear a path. Check on your neighbors. Find out whose cattle these were.* He showed one man how to tie a proper knot, another how to leverage a heavy load.

Then, he saw Marietta.

When she'd arrived, he had no idea, but she was here with her own Winchester. A heavy shawl coiled around her shoulders, and downy flecks of snow had gathered on her black hair. Clenching her jaw, she swept her gaze over the street and pressed her lips into a thin line.

She went straight to the mercantile, where a woman sobbed over a shattered storefront window. Putting an arm around her shoulders, Marietta spoke a few quiet words, then led her inside. A moment later, Marietta came back out with a broom and swept broken glass from the wooden walkway.

The rope went slack in Tate's hands as he watched her.

These people had all abandoned her three weeks ago, after the attack. Yet here she was, helping them put things to right. She really was the heart of this place.

Hopefully, the townsfolk will be smart enough to figure that out, too.

"Good day, Mr. Hollister."

Tate turned in the direction the voice had come from.

An older woman stood there. A gray woolen shawl covered her head and shoulders, and her hands, rough with work, clutched each other at her waist. She looked sturdy, like an oak that had weathered a lifetime of storms. She'd stood next to Nora at Marietta's uncle's funeral.

"Ma'am." He nodded and tipped his hat. "I remember you. From the churchyard."

"Adeleide McKenna. Nora's my girl." She looked him up and down. "Said you were a rancher."

"I was."

"And now?"

How am I supposed to answer that?

What *was* he now? A ghost? A hunter?

Just a man with nothing left to lose and a long list of debts to collect.

He gestured at the dead steer. "Right now, I'm haulin' a dead steer off the road."

"Did Marietta tell you she lost her folks when she was just a sprout?"

He shook his head.

"Everett was all the family she had left. That saloon ain't just wood and whiskey to her. It's the only home she's ever known." She took a step closer, lowering her voice. "She's a good girl, Mr. Hollister. But she's got a stubborn streak wider than the Brazos, and a fool notion she can carry this whole town on her own back."

He frowned. "You got a point, ma'am?"

Her eyes bored into him. "What are your intentions with her?"

Tate blinked; he'd never considered it. Intentions belonged to men who thought of futures and concerned themselves only with planting seasons and mending roofs.

What he had was a *purpose*—a nameless target with no face and a grave to fill.

"I intend to see the men who killed her uncle put in the ground."

Adeleide tilted her head, as though expecting more.

Tate let out a slow breath, the cold air stinging his lungs. "And to make sure no more harm finds its way to her door."

She held his gaze for a long moment.

He stood there, feeling like a horse being judged at auction, having its teeth and spirit examined for flaws.

Finally, Adeleide's face softened, the hard lines around her mouth relaxing as her shoulders eased.

"That's good to hear."

He huffed. "Reckon I just passed a test?"

"This town's been lost a long while. Folks are spooked. Don't know which way to look. They see a sheriff who's more concerned with the shine on his star than the iron on his hip. They needed a man to draw a line in the snow, and you did that today. For her... and for the rest of us."

He looked away from her.

She placed a hand on his arm. "Thank you."

With that, she walked away.

As she went, Tate looked around—really looked—past the immediate task of cleaning the street. The destruction and shattered windows. The townsfolk huddling together as their eyes darted to the empty plains, as if fearing that monsters would materialize from the storm to consume them.

A town on its knees.

Cade and Grady had joined Tate to chase their own personal revenge, but now, he realized this was bigger. He couldn't turn away from these people; he'd have to offer all he had to save the lives of these near strangers, just as Marietta had done for him.

Which meant Grady had been right: no more snooping through the woods, mud, and snow. The men he hunted didn't lurk in the wilderness—at least not *all* of them. How many skulked within the walls of Sherman itself, wearing the faces of neighbors and friends?

Well, Tate and his friends would just have to root them out. Rebuilding the ranch could wait. He'd stay with Marietta for as long as she'd have him, until he finished the job.

Marietta.

She'd moved on from the mercantile and now helped Mrs. Smith board up a broken window. Falling snow caught in the dark curls of her hair like tiny white stars in a midnight sky. Her small frame was as strong as the anvil in the smithy shop, yet even that strength paled before the force of her will.

He admired her.

Never thought I'd feel anything like that again.

Despite everything, all the pain and loss that had ravaged his soul, a current pulled him to her—a dangerous feeling bringing treacherous warmth to seep into a heart he'd long since boarded up as uninhabitable.

Gradually, the *swish* of a swinging rope swelled in his ears. The sight of thread against pale skin swam into focus. His muscles burned as though he'd just cut Lynda down and dug her a grave all over again.

Then, the world faded, swallowed by the awful silence that she'd left behind.

He could not—*would* not—go through that again. If he allowed another person to fill that empty space, then faced that kind of loss again…

What little was left of him would break.

Chapter Ten

The rich, dark scent of coffee dragged Tate from sleep, cutting through the stale air and promising a world beyond the four walls and lumpy mattress of his small room.

For a moment, he drifted in the twilight between dream and waking, thinking himself back in a different life—a warmer one—where a gentle hand would shake his shoulder and a soft voice would murmur his name.

Then, the ache in his side pulled him taut, reminding him of a swinging rope and a promise he still had to keep.

Groaning, he pushed himself up and swung his legs over the side of the bed. The wound still throbbed, but its fiery pain had banked to embers. Nora's new set of stitches held. He'd progressed from a man made of glass to one made of stiff leather.

That, I can work with.

After pulling on his shirt and pants, he strapped his gun belt around his hips, then made for the stairs. The hum of varied conversation rose to meet him as he descended, hushed but more prominent than anything he'd heard in this saloon since the night of the attack.

He paused on the last step and surveyed the room.

The place had come back to life. Men who, two days ago, had scurried into holes like rabbits now huddled at the tables, hunching over steaming mugs. Smith nursed a coffee at the bar, his big hands wrapped around the tin. Old Man Miller argued with a drover over a hand of cards.

The patrons spoke in low tones and glanced at the door every now and then, but they'd returned.

Then, his eyes found Marietta.

As she wiped the counter, her dark hair caught the light. A ghost of a bruise lingered high on her cheekbone with a faint purple shadow. She looked up, and when she caught sight of him, the weariness fell away from her face like a discarded mask. The corners of her lips pulled into a smile that lit her green eyes from within.

While she filled up a heavy mug and put some food on a plate, Tate made his way to the bar and took a seat.

"Figured you'd crawl on down sooner or later." She slid the mug and plate in front of him. "Eat. You look like a coyote chewed you up and spit you out halfway to Abilene."

He shook his head and laughed.

The plate held two fried eggs with yolks of perfect sunny-yellow and a thick slice of smoked ham. From the mug, the same aromatic steam that had woken him rose and tickled his nose. Amid the chaos of the last few days, he hadn't really noticed, but he hadn't eaten a proper homemade meal since before the war.

Not since... Lynda.

She'd always hummed when she cooked, and—though, admittedly, tuneless—the sound had always warmed their small cabin more thoroughly than any fire could. Now, after leaving her to fend for herself, Tate was sitting here, letting another woman put a plate of food in front of him.

He had no right to the comfort this food and coffee offered.

Still, he couldn't deny that it was *good*—the salt of the ham, the richness of the egg yolk, the bitter strength of the coffee—Marietta knew what she was doing, that much was certain.

Besides, he could give himself *some* slack. With the Bone Orchard Boys waiting out there, Tate needed to stay strong if he was to have a chance at seeing his purpose through. He might as well enjoy Marietta's cooking.

He huffed as he swallowed another bite.

You keep makin' up excuses, Hollister. You're eatin' food that's not Lynda's, and you love it.

Once he finished, he pushed the clean plate away and drained the last of his coffee. By this point, the crowd had thinned out, the morning patrons having made their way back to their shops and work, leaving only a few old timers in the corner.

After stacking the now-clean mugs in a pyramid, Marietta walked around the bar and approached Tate, wiping her hands on her apron.

"So…" She glanced at the Colt on his hip. "What's the plan?"

"Thinkin' I'll go have a word with the sheriff."

She scoffed. "What for? You'd get more sense barkin' at a knot."

"Maybe, but I still wanna see what he knows, if anything."

Marietta's jaw tightened. "Then I'll come with."

He pursed his lips. "Sure that's wise?"

She'd definitely insist on going—he knew her well enough not to expect anything else—but he felt he had a duty to *try* to keep her out of this mess as much as he could. He reasoned that, if he made a show of visiting the sheriff *alone*, it might distract whatever informants the gang had in town from Marietta and her saloon.

One swinging rope had been enough for him; he neither needed nor wanted to see another.

"Wise or not, I won't sit here twiddlin' my thumbs while you tangle yourself in trouble."

"It'd be safer for you—"

"Sure wasn't *safe* when they kicked in my door three weeks ago."

He slumped. "Marietta…"

"Don't you *Marietta* me, Tate Hollister!" she snapped, slapping her palm on the bar. "If you think I'm some fragile flower, you got less sense than a box of rocks."

For a long moment, the crackling fire and the distant *clang* of the blacksmith's hammer filled the saloon.

Finally, Tate let out a gusty sigh. As much as he wished otherwise, it was obvious that he could not force Marietta to remain safely tucked in her saloon.

"Alright." He nodded slowly. "But wear your iron and keep your eyes peeled."

She winked and stepped back. "You worry too much. Now, let's go rattle our sheriff's cage."

Untying her apron and hanging it on a peg, Marietta grabbed a heavy wool coat from behind the door. As she shrugged it on and slung her Winchester over it, Tate donned his own coat, then held the door for her.

They stepped out into the cold, and the creak of packed snow beneath their boots seemed to boom like the first steps of a vanguard marching to battle.

***

Unlike all the other buildings on the street, the sheriff's office had no festive greenery on its door. Its windows stared out like a pair of vacant eyes, the thin plume of smoke crawling from its chimney to vanish against the gray sky.

This building, which held itself separate from the town it supposedly served, smelled like a hostile fort in friendly country.

Tate pushed the door open without knocking.

Sitting behind a barricade of oak shaped like a desk, Sheriff Amos Sharpe looked up from a stack of papers seemingly too neat to be involved in any real work. The star on his chest reflected light like a mirror.

"Ms. Walker? What brings you by?" Sharpe glanced at Tate and frowned. "Hollister, you oughtta be restin'. Man in your shape has no business bein' out in this cold."

"We ain't here for pleasantries, Sheriff. We come to talk about the Bone Orchard Boys."

The sheriff held up a hand with clean nails. "I'm handlin' the situation."

"Handlin' it?" Marietta stepped forward. "They rode into town like they owned the place—butchered cattle right in the damn street!"

"Regrettable, to be sure," Sharpe drawled, leaning back in his chair, "but we can't go actin' rash without all the facts."

"That gang is bleedin' this county dry, and that's fact." Tate leaned his hands on the edge of the desk. "They shot me. They ambushed my friends. They killed Marietta's uncle."

"Yes, and—"

"What are you doing to find the man pulling the strings?"

Sharpe shuffled the papers on his desk. "We've caught a few before, just drifters, lowlifes—"

"I don't give a hoot about the thugs!" Tate pushed himself off the desk. "Snake don't die if you only cut off its rattle—you gotta take its head. What are you doin' to find the leader?"

The clock on the wall ticked like a hammer hitting a distant nail as Sharpe examined the tip of a quill as if it were the most interesting thing in the world.

Marietta crossed her arms. "Well, Sheriff?"

"This ain't some common outlaw, Marietta." Sharpe placed the quill down with exaggerated care. "This man is a phantom. A ghost who never shows his face and never leaves a trail. The men we capture know nothing, else they die before they can talk. I've spent months—years, even—looking for a name, a face, anything, but all I get is whispers in the wind."

The words tumbled out smoothly for Tate's liking, with the feel of a well-rehearsed speech. Sharpe painted a picture of an invisible mastermind, too clever to be caught by the likes of a simple country sheriff, and expected them to excuse his own idleness.

A man who *truly* hunted a ghost would have haunted eyes and calloused hands, not the placid face of a store clerk.

"My uncle is *dead*, Sheriff." Marietta glared at him. "And it weren't 'whispers' that killed him—so you'll forgive me if I don't much care for your excuses."

Sharpe raised his hands. "Now, I know you're hurtin', ma'am, but we gotta be careful. Wait for him to make a mistake."

Tate had heard generals say things like that during the war, old men in clean uniforms who sent boys to die in the mud while they studied maps miles from the fighting. They spoke of caution and strategy, words that, to Tate, had always smelled like a coward's justification for doing nothing.

"So we pull lint out of our ears while they butcher our stock, burn our homes, and kill our families." Tate scoffed. "That your plan?"

Sharpe stood and smoothed the front of his vest with his palm. "Only plan keeps the townsfolk safe."

Tate exchanged a look with Marietta. Her green eyes flashed with fire that could've melted lead, her hand resting on the stock of her Winchester.

He gave a slight shake of his head, and she let go of the gun. They'd get nothing more here, even if they tried to spook the lazy son of a gun into doing something for once.

"We'll see ourselves out." Tate turned for the door.

Marietta stomped out after him.

As they stepped out into the cold, the air came down like a fresh drink of water after the stale confines of the office. The heavy oak door shut behind them with a *thud*.

Packed snow squeaked under their feet as they walked.

From the awning of Miller's Mercantile, a snow-dusted string of dried apples and popcorn hung in a festive loop. A carved wooden star in the window of the smithy glowed with faint warmth from the forge within. Nearly every door displayed a simple wreath of pine boughs tied with a scrap of red cloth or twine, offering a silent greeting.

These people lived under the shadow of a gang that killed without reason, and the man who was supposed to protect them offered only empty words.

Yet here they were, stringing popcorn and hanging stars. Insisting on Christmas and facing the darkness with small acts of hope, refusing to let terror win.

Tate glanced at Marietta.

The wind had whipped color into her cheeks, and icy crystals dotted her dark hair like tiny diamonds as she looked at the decorations.

Watching her, Tate saw her expression soften for the first time since her uncle's death.

Chapter Eleven

A chair splintered against a support post with a *crack*, its legs flying across the room, yet the sound barely registered above the roared insults.

Jedediah Finn crashed against the piano, fishing a dissonant groan from the instrument's wires. Silas Cain was on him in a flash, flailing with fists as clumsy as sacks of grain. Whiskey sloshed from their tin mugs, painting dark circles that stank up the floorboards Marietta had just scrubbed that morning.

From behind the bar, she watched the two men grapple and grunt.

As always, it had started with a disagreement over a card game, but the fuel for this fire actually burned deeper.

The town *reeked* of fear. It soured the whiskey and turned good men into snarling dogs desperate to prove they still had teeth.

Another night, another pair of fools breaking my furniture to prove their grit.

She slammed a clean mug down on the bar, cutting through the din for a bare second before the fight swallowed it again.

"That's enough!"

Silas, a trickle of blood leaking from his nose, pushed Jedediah away and pointed a trembling finger. "He called me a yellow-bellied coward!"

"And I'll do it again!" Jedediah spat a wad of bloody phlegm onto the floor. "You seen 'em ridin' through town! Just sat there behind your window like a scared jackrabbit!"

Silas roared and jumped on Jedediah again.

Marietta clamped her hand around the shotgun that now lived propped against the back bar. The day Uncle Everett had taught her to shoot it, his big, warm hand guiding hers, the recoil had jarred her down to her bones. *Never point it unless you mean to use it, Etta-girl. A gun ain't a talkin' stick.*

Well, tonight it would have to do some talking.

She hefted it and moved from behind the bar. The sad collection of ranchers and townsfolk, who'd been watching the spectacle with a mixture of amusement and anxiety, shrank from her, parting like a river around a stone, glancing nervously at her shotgun's twin muzzles.

Marietta stopped a few feet from the brawling men. "That's *enough*, I said!"

Jedediah gave her a bleary look. "Ain't none o' your concern, Marietta."

"*Everything* that happens under this roof's my concern." She clenched the shotgun. "My tables, my piano, my damn floor! You best quit bustin' up my property and haul yourselves outta my saloon."

Silas snorted, wiping his bloody nose with the back of his hand. "Or what? You gonna shoot us?"

Don't tempt me.

She cocked both hammers of the shotgun. The dual *clicks* spoke a language every man in the room understood perfectly.

The last of the fight draining from them, Jedediah and Silas slumped their shoulders. The liquor-fueled rage in their eyes faded, leaving behind only bewildered shame.

"Now." She pointed the barrels at the floor between them. "I'll say it once more: *Get. Out.*"

They stumbled over each other in their haste to obey, grabbing their coats from a peg by the door. Without a backward glance, they pushed through the batwing doors and vanished into the snowy night, leaving broken furniture and the stench of their cowardice in their wake.

Marietta let out a slow breath she didn't realize she'd been holding.

The remaining patrons avoided her eyes, suddenly seeming to find their drinks intensely interesting. One by one, they drained their mugs, dropped coins on the tables, and shuffled out into the darkness until she stood, alone, amid the wreckage.

Shaking, she uncocked the hammers and leaned the shotgun back in its place.

She hated this—the weapon, that she'd had to use it, and the men who'd brought their violence to her door.

Uncle Everett would've handled them without ever touching his rifle. He would've planted his feet, crossed his great arms, and quelled the storm with a low rumble from his chest and a look from his stormy eyes.

Her, they just saw as a woman alone.

The corner table, where Uncle had liked to sit and read the newspaper, stood vacant. She could almost see his ghostly shape in the worn armchair, denting the cushion, the light from the window catching the gray in his mustache. He would've cleared his throat and turned the page, grumbling about something or other he'd read.

I'm so tired, Uncle... so tired of being strong.

Sweeping up shards of glass and splinters of wood, she felt the futility of it all press down on her. She could clean the floors and right the tables, but she couldn't fix what had broken in this town.

She couldn't sweep away the fear.

The search for the Bone Orchard Boys' leader had become a fool's errand. Cade spent his days watching Sheriff Sharpe, a thankless task that yielded nothing but confirmation of the man's profound laziness. Grady moved through the streets like a gentle giant, gauging the courage of his neighbors, only to report that their spines had dissolved like sugar in the rain.

And Tate...

Marietta stopped sweeping and leaned on the broom, her gaze gliding to the map tacked to the wall behind the bar. The spiderweb of dead ends and crossed-out leads on its surface gave testament to their failure. Tate had sat with her for hours, tracing the lines with his dark eyes and murmuring as they went over the same useless facts again and again.

He was doing everything he could; she knew that. He had his own ghosts, which lived in the set of his jaw and the haunted quiet that occasionally claimed him. Though he hadn't shared its origins with her, his need for vengeance burned as hot as her own.

Yet she couldn't bring herself to truly lean on him. She couldn't place her hope, safety, and entire world into his hands.

Trust was a currency she no longer possessed.

She'd spent it all on graves.

She'd *trusted* her parents to come home from that trip to Dallas. Robert to come back from the war. The earth on Uncle's grave still hadn't settled.

Everyone she'd ever truly relied on, she'd lost. They'd left holes in her life, ragged-edged voids that ached with the cold. How could she risk creating another?

So she let Tate help. Listened to his plans and nodded at his theories, but deep inside, in a place she kept walled off and guarded, she knew she had to do this herself.

Just then, a gust of wind drove a swirl of fine snow across the floorboards she'd just swept as the batwing doors groaned open.

Marietta looked up, already reaching for the shotgun, then found Nora and Adeleide standing on the threshold.

"Figured we'd let you breathe a bit before comin' over." Nora unwound her scarf as she stepped inside. "How're you holdin' up?"

"I'm fine." Marietta kicked a stray chair leg out of her path. "Just another Tuesday night at the Walker Saloon."

Adeleide closed the door behind them, shutting out the rising moan of the wind. "'Fine' is a word for people who ain't just chased two grown men outta their place of business with a scattergun."

"I—"

"Hush, child." Adeleide smiled. "Ain't no shame in acceptin' a hand. Nora, sugar—put that kettle on."

Marietta wanted to refuse, to insist she didn't need their fussing, but the fight had leached the strength from her bones. Her knees trembled as if she'd carried a boulder up a mountain. She slumped into a chair at the one unscathed table.

As Nora stepped into the kitchen, Adeleide sat opposite Marietta.

"Go on, then." Adeleide put her palms on the table. "Tell me what's eatin' at ya."

"C'mon, don't tell me you didn't see the whole thing."

"Me seein' it don't draw the poison outta your heart."

"Neither will talkin' about things we all already know."

Adeleide chuckled. "You'd be surprised."

"Adeleide—"

"Just hush and start talking."

Marietta looked away and sighed. "I'm sick of it—the hollerin' and spit, the puffed-up pride. They call each other cowards while the whole town's gettin' chewed to pieces by wolves, and expect me to keep pourin' whiskey and mop up their mess!"

"It will pass."

"Will it?" Marietta threw her hands up. "We ain't got nothin'! We're chasing shadows, staring at that damn map till our eyes ache—and for what? The trail's colder than a well-digger's toes, and the one man with a badge sits polishin' it, preachin' *patience*."

"Patience *is* a virtue, Marietta."

"It's a *stone* that drags you to drown while you wait for help that never comes." Marietta leaned forward. "Uncle Everett was a good man, a strong man, and they gunned him down behind his own bar!"

Even after watching him bleed out on the floor, Marietta still imagined him alive and laughing, his mustache hiding the curve of his smile as he told her one of his old stories.

He hadn't made a sound as he'd died—not one shout, yelp, or groan—yet, as the thin keen of the kettle drifted from the kitchen, it sounded *exactly* like a scream.

Whether Uncle's or hers, Marietta could only guess.

Adeleide reached across the table and covered Marietta's hand with her own. "You gotta let that anger settle, child, especially with the storm comin' on."

Marietta blinked. "What?"

"Trappers come through this mornin', saying a big one's brewing in the mountains." Adeleide shook her head. "Blizzard, worse than the last, by tomorrow night. Could hang around a few days."

Days—trapped—snow piling up against the doors and windows, sealing them in this tomb of a town.

"No—no, we were fixin' to ride out again. Tate and Cade were checkin' that old line cabin near the river."

Action—doing something, *anything*—had been the one thread of hope that kept her sanity from unraveling. Now, the sky *itself* conspired against her; as if to confirm Adeleide's news, wind howled outside, rattling the windowpanes.

Like a trapped animal, Marietta had been chewing her own leg off to get out of her snare, only to find out the hunter had built a wall around the whole forest.

She wanted to *scream* again, to *smash* something, to punch sky.

Her head snapped up as the batwing doors creaked open again, admitting Tate and Cade. Snow clung to their shoulders and the brims of their hats.

Tate nodded at her as he hung his hat, and the fire in her chest receded a few inches.

For weeks, they'd been sharing little moments: a glance over the map, a brush of fingers as he took a plate from her, a quiet minute by the hearth. He hadn't fixed a single broken thing in her life, but his presence had made everything a little easier to bear, and now, he calmed her just by coming in.

She exhaled slowly.

Cade took off his hat and slapped it against his leg, sending a shower of snowflakes to the floor. "Smells like you had some trouble here."

"Nothing I couldn't handle."

Tate's eyes lingered on the splintered post, then moved back to her. He raised an eyebrow.

A wry twist tugging her lips, she gave him a little shrug. *I'm fine, really.*

"Line cabin was empty." Tate came over to her table and sat between her and Adeleide. "Tracks headed south a few days back, but the snow buried what's left."

Of course. She'd expected nothing better than another dead end, another failure, and now, a blizzard was rushing in to engulf their hopes completely.

BOOM

The saloon doors crashed open and slammed into the walls with enough force to shake the building.

A figure in a snow-caked buffalo coat and a wide-brimmed hat pulled low stumbled into the room. Wind and snow roared behind him in a white vortex that extinguished both lamps on the far wall, plunging half the room into shadow.

Tate's Colt appeared in his hand, and Cade drew his pistol. They jumped up and flanked the intruder while Marietta rushed for her shotgun.

The stranger, leaner than Grady but wider than Tate, slumped against the doorframe, then thumped forward until he collapsed on the floor. As he sagged and breathed with ragged clouds of steam, the doors swung shut behind him.

He pushed his hat back with his index finger bent at a sharp angle. Deep lines stretched around hazel eyes, and snow and frost coated his brown beard. He held his free hand against his side...

Where a dark stain pooled across the thick wool of his coat.

Chapter Twelve

Tate could not believe his eyes.

A dead man had stumbled out of the storm because the sheriff's deputy had found *this* man in the snow with a bullet in his back. Either the lawman had lied, or—more likely—hadn't even been to the cabin in the first place.

Tate lowered the barrel of his pistol. "Fletcher?"

"Tate..." The ghost of Fletcher Avery panted amid a heap of wet buffalo hide and shuddering limbs. "Mind givin' a fella a hand?"

Tate gestured to Cade, and together, they hauled Fletcher up and half-carried, half-dragged him to the table, then dumped him into a chair. He slumped forward, head lolling, crimson dripping onto the clean-swept floor beneath him to spread like a spiderweb across the wood grain.

Nora pushed them aside, opening her leather satchel. "Get this coat off him. Marietta, I need hot water and clean rags."

While Marietta moved to the kitchen, Nora took a pair of shears to the thick buffalo hide, snipping through the tough material with sharp *clicks*. Tate leaned over the table, planting his hands on either side of Fletcher, and stared into the man's unfocused eyes. The smell of pine, wet wool, and old blood filled his nostrils.

"The deputy said you were dead."

Fletcher blinked. "Well, they sure as hell *tried* to get rid of me."

Cade stood beside Tate. "What in blazes were you doin' at that cabin anyhow?"

"I *wasn't*." Fletcher groaned. "I was ridin' that way when them bastards come tearin' after me."

Nora peeled back the last of the coat and the bloody shirt beneath. She pressed a cloth to Fletcher's side, and he hissed through his teeth. Tate examined the ragged tear of flesh, high on the ribs, and grimaced.

Looks the same as mine.

"How'd they know we were coming, Fletcher?" Tate leaned closer. "Even if we never told you when we'd do it, you were the only one who knew our plan."

"I don't know..." Fletcher's head sagged. "I swear to God, Hollister. Ain't breathed a word to no livin' soul."

The memory of the ambush flared behind Tate's eyes. Muzzle flashes blooming like hellish flowers in the churning snow. The phantom kick of the bullet throwing him against the rock. They'd ridden into a slaughterhouse because of this man.

Because he'd told them where to go.

"Save your snake oil for someone else," Cade growled. "First, they damn near gun us all down, then you vanish. A month later, deputy says you're pushin' daisies—and now, you come draggin' in? You figure we'll shake your hand and call it even, just 'cause you're bleeding?"

"I'm tellin' you straight!" Fletcher coughed. "They must've found out I pointed you their way somehow—they spent a month chasin' me through the all-fired wilderness!"

"Please, spare us! How can you—"

"I'm a *rancher*, not a trapper, Cade!" Fletcher breathed hard. "Try livin' on tree bark and snowmelt a whole month, then see how *your* teeth feel!"

Nora, having cleaned the wound of grime and dirt during the heated exchange, now brandished a poultice redolent of yarrow and wintergreen. "You got lucky. The ball went clean through—took some meat with it, but you'll live."

Lucky.

Tate hated that word. Luck was for cardsharps and fools. Out here, you made your own fate with a quick eye and a steady hand. Fletcher Avery's *luck* smelled like the yarn a man spun after he sold out his friends for a handful of silver, then got cheated out of his payment.

"C'mon, Fletcher, be honest with yourself." Tate sat down. "You must know what this sounds like."

"Go kick rocks, you mule-headed—"

"He could be tellin' the truth."

Blinking, Tate turned.

Marietta stood by the end of the table, holding a basin of steaming basin, her green eyes moving between Fletcher and Tate.

Tate blinked. "What you mean?"

"Maybe it *wasn't* him." She placed the basin on the table with a soft *clink*. "You said yourself that someone in this town must be working with them."

"Yeah—and we're starin' right at him!"

"You sure no one else knew?"

Cade sat down, too. "We were careful, Marietta."

"That right?" She dried her hands on her apron. "So, you met him at home? Never spoke in public?"

Tate frowned.

When they'd overheard Fletcher complaining to Sharpe about strange men on his land, none of them had wanted him anywhere near their ranches until they learned more about him. After two years of gathering rumors and clues, paranoia had settled in, making anyone and everyone a suspect.

Consequently, they'd spoken to Fletcher on the street, in front of Miller's Mercantile—in hushed tones, of course, but out in the open, nonetheless. Fletcher had drawn a crude map in the snow with the toe of his boot. Anyone with eyes could've seen it. From the window of Miller's Mercantile. The blacksmith's shop. Even a wagon passing in the street.

But no one could have known what they were looking at... right?

Now, however, Tate wasn't so sure.

His mind raced, dredging up memories of what, at the time, he'd thought was a sufficiently covert exchange. Who'd been watching them as they huddled together, heads bent in conspiracy?

Old Man Miller had been sweeping his porch, occasionally glancing their way over the top of his spectacles. Pike, the cattleman, had been leaning against a post and whittling, maybe a little *too* engrossed in shaping the scrap of wood. Even Sharpe's useless deputy had given them a long look as he stalked past, ostensibly on patrol.

The whole blasted town could have been watching. Anyone could've overheard a stray word, seen a pointed finger, and—with enough information—put the pieces together.

Looking at Marietta, Tate shook his head reluctantly. "There *were* people around."

Fletcher snorted. "Damn right, there were."

"You said you were riding 'that way' when the outlaws came after you." Adeleide leaned forward. "What does that mean?"

Fletcher looked at her. "I went back to the cabin that night."

A bitter taste, like old coffee grounds, coated Tate's tongue. A man did not go back to a hornet's nest he'd just pointed out to others.

Unless he means to watch the hornets work.

Tate stiffened. "Why in God's name would you do somethin' that fool-headed?"

"Got a bad feelin'." Fletcher shook his head. "Guessed you boys were fixin' to make a move, and the blizzard... it was too perfect a cover."

Cade raised an eyebrow. "So, you just rode out into that gale on a *feelin'*?"

"Didn't ride in close. Left my horse in a draw half a mile west, then went the rest on foot, hugging trees, and let the storm do the hidin' for me. Wanted one last look, just to make sure the odds hadn't changed none."

Tate searched the lines around Fletcher's hazel eyes for a lie; all he found was exhaustion and the haunted expression only hunger and cold could leave. A man could fake many things, but *not* the look of someone who'd spent a month staring into the frozen teeth of winter and barely escaped its bite.

"Well?" Tate leaned in. "What did you see?"

Fletcher took a shuddering breath. "Two men came out on the porch, standin' under that little overhang, tryin' to keep the snow off their hats. They talked close, like men with secrets."

Nora finished her last stitch, tied off the thread with a firm tug, and covered the wound with her fragrant poultice, then wrapped it off with clean dressings.

"Did you recognize 'em?"

"One of 'em, yeah—Ransom Calder."

Calder?

Tate knew that name from rumbling talk at cattle auctions and saloons from here to the Red River. Calder traveled with whispers of burned-out homesteads and ranchers who suddenly decided to sell their land for a song. Folks said he was a foreman for some big outfit back east, a man who got things done, no matter the cost.

"Mean as a snake with a busted tail, that one." Fletcher's gaze fell to the tabletop. "Came to my spread a few months back with two hired guns. Said I had a fine piece of land. Be a shame if it caught fire or if I went 'missin'.' Offered me pennies on the dollar to sell. I told him he could go to hell and take his boots with him."

Marietta moved from the end of the table and stood behind Tate, placing a hand on his back.

"And the other man?" Tate tapped the table. "Who was with Calder?"

"Can't say. Fella was slick—kept his hat low and a bandana right up to his eyes. Never caught his face, but he weren't no ordinary saddle tramp."

Cade tilted his head. "What makes you say that?"

"Weren't no even trade o' words. Calder acted like a whipped dog givin' a report to the man with the leash. I heard scraps through the wind—somethin' about control, squeezin' the town dry, buyin' up ranches cheap—that kind o' talk."

Tate clenched his fist. "So, you're sayin'…"

Fletcher nodded. "Calder was takin' orders. The man with the bandana, whoever he was, outranked him."

Everything fit like a bullet in the chamber of a gun.

That masked man had to be the leader. With how bad the snowstorm had been that night, the leader would've needed to be present to effectively organize the counterattack, and neither Tate, Cade, nor Grady had gotten close enough to peek inside the cabin. That filthy snake could've just sat in there, drinking whiskey, while his men shot at Tate and his friends in the snow.

"They talked about sellin' the ranches to the highest bidder." Fletcher's voice gained strength. "That, with the ranchers scared off and the town on its knees, they could name their price."

Marietta squeezed Tate's shoulder. "How'd they spot you?"

"Your guess is as good as mine. Must've snapped a twig or stepped wrong. Bandana-man looked up right at me and pointed. Next thing I knew, bullets were singin' past my ears."

After that, the rest of Fletcher's story tumbled out. He spoke of riding crashing through the timber after him while the blizzard raged, then how he doubled back, using the storm to cover his tracks, and burrowed into a snowdrift, praying they'd ride past.

He'd circled back toward civilization, only to find riders patrolling the perimeter of town, watching the roads. So he'd stayed in the wilderness, eating roasted squirrel and meltwater.

For a month, he'd lived like an animal.

He described gnawing hunger, nights spent shivering in makeshift shelters, and the constant fear that every gust of wind carried the sound of approaching hoofbeats.

As Tate listened, the last of his suspicions dissolved.

A liar told a clean story, a simple one; an honest man, though, remembered each and every small, miserable detail: the ache in his teeth and the knot of fire twisting his stomach after days with no food.

Tate had lived that life in the war, and he recognized its bitter taste in Fletcher's words.

"They finally caught up to me yesterday, near the river." Fletcher shuddered. "Must've found my tracks. I was tired, careless. They didn't even say a word—just rode up, and Calder... he *smiled*. Right before he shot me."

Tate nodded. "How'd you live through it?"

"They left me to bleed out in the snow, that's how. Reckon they figured the cold and coyotes would finish the job." Fletcher drew in a ragged breath. "After they rode off, I waited. I don't know how long. An hour, maybe a whole day. Then, I started crawlin'. I knew I wouldn't make it to my own spread, so I came here, lookin' for Old Everett."

"Oh..." Marietta looked down. "You don't know..."

As she related what had happened to her uncle, Tate looked at the crackling fire.

They had a name now—Ransom Calder—and a ghost in a bandana. Of course, with the storm looming, they'd be trapped in Sherman.

But for the first time in two years, Tate had more than just faceless phantoms.

Chapter Thirteen

As the world outside surrendered to the approaching storm, wind wailed like a mother weeping for her lost child.

Inside, the scent of whiskey and wood smoke pressed on Marietta's shoulders. The fire in the stone hearth had collapsed into a bed of embers that pulsed with dull light.

Marietta traced the rim of her empty mug. Across the table, Tate sat with his shoulders hunched, a silhouette carved of shadow and firelight, and stared into the glowing embers.

For hours, they'd sat like two sentinels guarding a tomb while the town slept through the gathering storm. Nora and Adeleide had long since bundled up and braved the first flurries to get home, leaving Fletcher Avery sleeping off a dose of laudanum upstairs, his snores rumbling through the floorboards.

Marietta shook her head. *A dead man sleepin' in my guest room.*

The whole blasted world had turned upside down.

"Feller's out colder'n a creek stone in January." She set her mug down on the rough-hewn wood. "Hard to figure how a man can snore like that after all he's been through."

Tate picked up his own mug, then set it down again. "He's breathin'. That's more grace than he earned."

"That tale he spun about Calder and that bandana-wearin' bastard... It gives us somethin', leastways. A face. A name to chew on."

"All it gives us is *yarn*." Tate glanced at the map behind the bar. "Makes him look like some poor sucker and us the chuckleheaded fools who didn't take heed."

"You said it yourself—ain't hard for folks to see who's jawin' in the street." She leaned forward. "One man sweepin' his stoop, another whittlin' a stick... word slips out easy as breath. Ain't his fault this town's got ears like a barn owl."

For her part, Marietta *wanted* to believe Fletcher. Lord, she needed to believe in *something*, in a new lead, a broken link in the gang's chain. Hope was a dangerous thing, a flickering candle in a gale, but it was all she had left to warm her hands on. Even if trusting Fletcher amounted to betting her last coin on cards she hadn't seen, she had to do it.

"We'll keep eyes on him." Tate tapped the wood. "He bunks here, where we can see whether he's a snake or a hen, eats our grub, sleeps under our rafters—he don't set a boot outside without one of us knowin' about it."

Marietta nodded.

Her eyes followed Tate's to the dark cross on the map that marked the trapper's cabin. From that single point, all this ruin had flowed. It had consumed her uncle, nearly killed Tate, and now, it held Sherman in its coils, squeezing tighter with every passing day.

"How does a man stay a ghost in a town this small?"

"Come again?"

"Can't buy a boot around here without ol' Miller knowin' your size. How can one spider spin so many strings, yet keep his web hidden all the while?"

Tate's chair groaned as he shifted to look back at the embers for several moments before he spoke.

"Some generals never saw a speck of mud in the war." Orange light glinted in the depths of his eyes. "Sat in clean tents, miles from hell, pushin' pins on maps while boys bled out in the muck. Sent runners to carry their killin' orders."

"Don't rightly explain how this one's pullin' it off so slick-like."

"Whoever runs his errands ain't no rifle-totin' thug. Could be some street kid, could be Miller, could be Smith, for all we know." Tate pried a loose splinter from the table and turned it over in his rough fingers. "Could even be a dog, if it's smart enough. Don't take a genius to tote a note."

Marietta looked at Tate. Really looked at him—not just as a wounded stranger or grim-faced ally, but as a man.

Firelight carved deep shadows under his cheekbones and picked out the gray beginning to frost the dark hair at his temples. He waged his own war inside him; it lived in the hard set of his jaw and the quiet that clung to him like a second skin. Yes, he'd brought this fight to her door, but he'd also *stayed*—stood with her in the wreckage, organized men in the street, and lent his own strength to her crumbling world.

But why?

Yes, his ranch lay in ashes. A terrible thing, a loss that would break most men. She'd seen it happen: ranchers lost their spreads to fire, drought, or bad luck, then packed their wagons and moved on, looking for a new start.

But men like that didn't spend two years hunting those responsible like wolves on a blood trail.

There was a difference between seeking restitution and wanting a reckoning, and Tate thirsted for the latter. No, this went deeper than burned wood and scattered stock. Whatever dark current ran beneath his calm surface, whatever pain he bore, she *had* to know.

She yearned to understand the shape of the man who now sat at the center of her life, who'd become the fulcrum on which her future—and her vengeance—now turned.

Marietta folded her hands on the table as the wind shrieked, rattling the windowpane as if seeking entry. She met Tate's dark gaze across their small island of light in the vast dark of the saloon.

"Tate." She inhaled. "Why are you doin' this?"

He frowned. "What you mean?"

"The Bone Orchard Boys." She exhaled. "Time you quit skirtin' around it and tell me what those devils truly did to you."

He picked up the splinter again, rubbing his thumb carelessly over its sharp edges.

"Two years back, I dragged myself home from the war. Walked near half the country with one thought in my head: Lynda." The name caught in his throat like a shard of glass he couldn't swallow. "My wife. That spread weren't just boards an' dirt. It was our promise. Our piece of quiet carved out from all the thunder."

Marietta held her breath.

"House was gutted when I got there—torn to hell—but it weren't no robbery." He looked up. "They dragged her out to the big oak, the same one we got hitched under. Used a rope, like she was nothin' but cattle."

Marietta's fingers grew cold, and she wrapped them around her coffee mug, looking for warmth no longer there.

"Cade found me there. He'd just put his wife and two little gals in the ground. Same bastards, same day. Grady hid his kin in the root cellar, but they got his folks and brother while he listened from the dark, helpless as a boy."

He tossed the splinter onto the table.

"Weren't never 'bout a burned spread. Not really. We made a pact, us three: no rest 'til the bastard who ordered his dogs to tear through good folk was layin' six feet under the dirt he wanted so bad."

"Tate, I..."

He smiled crookedly. "Reckon that makes four of us now, don't it?"

"I'm sorry for your loss." She looked down. "I—I lost someone too. My fiancé."

Tate put his palm on hers and nodded.

"His name was Robert. We grew up together. He wanted to be a doctor."

She looked down at her hands, at the calluses from scrubbing floors and hefting barrels, and remembered the soft touch of Robert's hands. They'd been meant for healing.

"The war?"

"Yeah." She closed her eyes for a moment. "Letters quit comin' after a while, but I waited, fool that I am. Then, a note showed up from his captain. Said he died at some hellhole called Cold Harbor. Claimed it was quick, but..."

She'd never believed that part.

"I'm sorry for your loss."

"After that…" She shrugged. "I never saw the point in wishing for anyone else, like even considering it would be a betrayal. No use trying to fill a space that was shaped only for him, anyway. Uncle Everett was all I had left."

After a moment, Tate spoke again. "My folks been gone a long while. I weren't nothin' but a kid. Comanche raiding party tore through our place—land squabble, same damn story from one end o' the territory to the other." He turned his hands over on the table, revealing palms crossed with scars. "They killed them all. My ma, my pa, my baby sister."

The fire popped, sending a fresh shower of sparks up the chimney. A fist of wind hammered the window, and snow hissed against the glass. The air grew thick and warm. Heat radiated from his skin to hers.

Then, Tate's gaze dropped to her mouth, and a shudder traced a path down her spine.

The scent of him—woodsmoke, coffee, and the clean smell of the winter air that clung to his clothes—filled her senses as he leaned forward, just a fraction of an inch.

Without thinking, she did the same. Her lips parted. The thought of his touch, the rough scrape of his beard against her skin, the solid warmth of his lips, sent a jolt through her belly.

Suddenly, he jerked back as if the fire had leapt from the hearth and burned him, then stood and stepped back. His chair scraped against the floorboards with a harsh shriek. The warmth in his eyes vanishing, he turned away and ran a hand through his dark hair.

"It's late. We need to be up before dawn. Lots of work to do tomorrow, clearin' my spread, now that the storm's moving in."

What?

"Goodnight, Marietta."

He made his way up the stairs quickly, as though fleeing a pack of feral dogs.

Marietta stared at the dark into which he'd vanished. The embers in the hearth mocked her, and their warmth faded into cold ash, even as a hot flush crept up her neck and burned her cheeks.

What just happened?

He'd looked at her and leaned in. She hadn't imagined that, had she? There was no way she'd spun it all from wishful thinking or conjured a daydream from shared sorrow and the late hour. He *had* been about to kiss her... hadn't he?

Of course not. You're crazy for thinkin' he might actually be interested.

Tate had buried his heart in a cold grave next to his wife, and truthfully, Marietta was no different. Literally moments before, she'd told him she wasn't looking to replace Robert. What right did she have to feel the sting of rejection, this ridiculous, childish bruise on her pride?

It would be a bad idea, anyway—a terrible, dangerous notion—to let any kind of affection for Tate Hollister take root in the barren ground of her heart. Sentiment bred vulnerability, and she could not afford to create another window for the world to break and let the cold in.

She stood and pushed her chair in with more force than necessary.

The mission—that was all that mattered—the map on the wall, Ransom Calder, and the ghost in the bandana. She'd take the hurt and confusion, the memory of that almost-kiss, and bank them to use as fuel for the fight ahead.

No, she wouldn't think about the look in Tate's eyes or the warmth that had bloomed in her chest for one foolish moment.

No distractions.

Chapter Fourteen

Tate kicked at a lump of charcoal that had once been a porch step, where Lynda used to sit and shell peas. The small *clunk-tink-clunk* it produced as it skittered across the frozen ground sounded far too loud.

He'd brought Cade out here under the pretense of scavenging for anything that might have survived the fire—tools, maybe a cast-iron pot—but the truth coiled in Tate's gut like a leaden snake. He'd *needed* to see this, to stand in his own graveyard and remind himself what happened when he forgot himself.

Like last night.

He'd sat across from Marietta in the warm lamplight of her saloon and, for a moment, let himself imagine kissing her. Her scent—a mix of soap and something he couldn't quite put his finger on, but that was hers alone—had filled his head, overwhelming the constant smell of old blood and gunpowder.

And logic.

She'd pulled him in like a warm current sweeping ice from a creek, drawing him forward with the slight part of her lips and the sparkle of her green eyes in the firelight. A man shouldn't plant a new crop on salted earth, yet there he'd been, ready to kiss her—right then and there—and consequences be damned.

The memory of Lynda's boots dangling above the snow had brought him to his senses, saving him from making that mistake.

A few feet away, Cade nudged a twisted piece of metal with the toe of his boot. "Ain't nothin' here but ghosts."

"No harm in takin' a look-see."

"Unless we freeze our hides off doin' it."

"Quit your bellyachin'." Tate shoved his hands deep into his pockets, brushing his knuckles against the extra bullets he always carried. "We'll head back before the sky really starts spittin' ice."

"I'd prefer to skip the whole dad-blamed blizzard, if it's all the same." Cade raised an eyebrow. "I'll cut you some slack, though. Sharper the cold bites now, sweeter whiskey'll bite later."

Tate grunted. *Marietta* would be the one serving them whiskey.

Cade just had to go and remind him of her—though, admittedly, he couldn't have known it.

In any case, the last thing Tate wanted to think about was Marietta. He meant to stand here and let the cold seep into his bones until his heart went numb. He'd come here for penance and a reminder of *why* he couldn't let his emotions get the better of him again, and Cade was spoiling it all with his doggone common sense.

Then, it got worse.

"You an' Marietta been gettin' chummy these days," Cade remarked, leaning against the cabin's burned wall. "Thick as thieves, you two."

Tate's jaw tightened until his teeth ached. "Don't start flappin' that tongue, Cade."

"Hey, I'm just sayin'—"

Tate rounded on him and pinned him with a glare. "I ain't in the mood."

"Growl all you please, but any fool with eyes can see it, plain as sunrise." Cade tipped his hat back. "When you reckon nobody's watchin', you look at her like she's the first fire you seen after a year-long winter."

"You ain't seen nothin'."

Tate turned his back on Cade and stalked toward the remains of the barn, where the great support beams had collapsed inward in a tangled mess of blackened wood.

Cade's boots crunched in the snow behind him.

"The *hell* I ain't—and I seen her sizin' you up, too. Woman's tougher'n rawhide, but around you, that steel softens right up."

Tate ran a gloved hand over a charred beam, dirtying the leather with greasy soot.

"You don't know what you're talkin' about."

"I know I put my wife an' my girls in the ground same day you laid Lynda down."

"Cade—"

"I *know* the feelin', Tate. Walkin' around with a hole in your chest big enough for the wind to whistle clean through."

"Then why—"

"'Cause you gone and built yourself a stone fort around that pain and set a sentry at the gate."

Tate whirled on him. "And what the hell d'you reckon I should do, huh? Throw open the gates an' show her the graveyard rottin' inside me? She's haulin' her own burden—she don't need to shoulder mine, too!"

"Maybe she *wants* to shoulder some of it—and you can take a bit o' hers! Ain't that what folks do when the world tries to break 'em?" Cade took a step closer. "You honestly think Lynda'd want you to drift through life like a ghost, too scared of your own shadow to let a decent woman close?"

Lynda's name knocked the air from Tate's lungs. He itched to hit something, to swing at Cade, at the burned timbers, at the uncaring sky. Instead, he clenched his fists in his pockets until his nails bit into his palms.

"You leave her out of this."

"What happened to Lynda ain't an excuse to turn away a chance for happiness when it comes knockin'. Marietta Walker is a chance, Tate, a *real* one. She puts a light in your eyes I ain't seen since before we went off to that godforsaken war."

A light? A bitter laugh scraped its way up Tate's throat.

Maybe so, but only a *fool's* light—a reflection of the fire that burned in her, and nothing more. He was a hollow man, a vessel for vengeance and nothing else. Last night had proved it. The moment a flicker of real feeling had sparked inside him, his past had risen up and smothered it.

"We're tied by a common cause. That's all. When this is done, I'm gone."

"And where you gonna go?" Cade threw his hands up. "This is your home! Or it was. You think ridin' off into the sunset will solve a damn thing? You'll just take your ghosts with you. They pack light for travel."

Just 'cause you're right, don't change a damned thing.

A man who'd brought death to his own family, gotten his best friend killed, and hadn't been able to protect his own wife didn't deserve a second chance. He hadn't earned the warmth in Marietta's smile or the trust in her eyes.

He was a curse walking on two legs.

Pushing past Cade, Tate walked back to the ruin of the house, but kicked something half-buried in snow and soot as he went. His wounded side pulled at him as he bent down, brushed the snow away, and picked up a piece of wood...

From the cradle he'd built in anticipation of the child he and Lynda had wanted. He'd carved it from good oak and sanded it smooth with his own two hands.

Flames had gnawed at it, leaving one of the rockers splintered and black, but looking down, he made out the faint shape of the star he'd carved into the headboard.

His hand twitched convulsively around the piece of scorched wood.

"Tate, I'm just sayin'..." Cade came up and put a hand on Tate's shoulder. "Don't let what you lost make you lose what you might find."

The blackened wood bit into Tate's palm as he squeezed until splinters threatened to pierce his glove, as if that pain could somehow ease the ache in his chest. Spinning around, he thrust the wood at Cade.

"And what about you, huh?" He jabbed the tip into Cade's chest. "You stand there, preachin' like some saint on a mountaintop, but I see you with Nora. The way you find a reason to be wherever she is. Maybe you oughtta spend less time mendin' *my* fences and tend to your own."

"Might be you're right," Cade admitted, shrugging, "but this ain't about me and—"

"The hell it ain't! It's about you tellin' me how to live when your own damn house ain't in order!"

"All I know is, a man don't get this riled up over somethin' he don't care about. You can stand here 'til hell freezes over and say it's just a common cause between you and her, but you're lookin' at me like you want to tear my head off just for sayin' her name."

Gathering a fresh volley of curses and deflections, Tate opened his mouth to retort, to peel back Cade's own raw grief over his lost family to remind him that *neither* of them deserved a second chance. Tate would tell him that Nora deserved better than a ghost, and so did Marietta, and that was the end of it. He would—

A low vibration in the soles of his boots stole the words from his mouth.

Cade frowned. "What's that?"

The vibration swelled from a tremor to an audible rumble, like a distant rockslide or a river breaking its frozen banks. But no, this sound had a cadence to it.

Hoofbeats.

Many hooves, drumming against the hardpan hidden beneath the snow, coming fast.

Tate grabbed his Colt. "Get down."

Tate and Cade dropped behind a collapsed wall, a low barricade of charred logs and stone that offered the only decent cover in the entire ruined spread. Snow whipped into their faces, stinging Tate's eyes as Cade levered a round into the chamber of his Winchester.

Dread quickened Tate's pulse; it had to be Ransom Calder and his men, come to pick through the ashes of Tate's life and salt the earth for good measure. Maybe Fletcher was a plant after all, a Judas goat meant to send word the moment Tate and Cade rode out alone.

Tate pressed his cheek against soot-covered stone and peered through a gap in the fallen logs.

They came from the trees, spreading out in a disciplined line as they cleared the woods: riders on lean ponies, churning through the snow as if it were dust. Except...

They didn't wear heavy wool coats, but fur-layered parkas over skin of burnished copper.

Breath burned in Tate's throat. Under his skin, heat simmered into an inferno as the smell of burned pine intensified around him—no longer that of a cabin put to the torch a month ago, but the aroma of a fire from a lifetime ago.

Memories he'd buried fourteen years ago surged to the front of his mind.

His mother shrieking. Soldiers dragging him away from the sight of her blood on the porch. His father lying prone by the woodpile, a constellation of arrows sprouting from his body. Sarah's swaddling soaked in red that had nothing to do with dye.

Bile rose in his throat. His knuckles whitened on the grip of the Colt.

The riders fanned out into a wide crescent, effectively sealing off any route of escape. Their ponies danced and snorted, their breath pluming in the frigid air. The harsh lines carved into every man who survived the frontier stretched across their faces. This was no raiding party of young bucks; these were seasoned Comanche warriors.

At their center, a tall man rode slightly ahead, his shoulders stretching the seams of his hide shirt. A red-tipped eagle feather tipped rose from his long black hair. Dark, deep-set eyes bore into Tate and Cade's hiding spot from crevices in his angular face.

"Comanche." Cursing, Cade spat on the ground. "Holy hell, Tate… Must be two dozen of 'em."

Resting his forearm on the charred log, Tate raised his Colt.

One clean shot. One pull of the trigger.

It would be the beginning of a bloodbath, a suicidal stand against impossible odds, but it would be worth it to appease the screaming wraiths in his head—payment, however small, on a debt that had festered for fourteen years.

His finger tightened on the trigger.

The Comanche leader raised an open hand, palm out. The riders behind him halted, their ponies tossing their heads in a restless line of muscle and steam. Then, he urged his buckskin forward, breaking from the line, and approached the ruined cabin alone.

Cade shifted beside Tate. "What's he doin'?"

"I…" Tate frowned. "I think he means to talk."

Chapter Fifteen

"This here's my land." Tate eased off the trigger but kept the Colt up. "That gives me every right to put a bullet through the first man so much as *twitches* wrong."

The leader slid from his pony and landed on the snow with a soft *crunch*. Walking forward, he raised both hands and stopped a dozen yards from the ruined cabin.

"I come not to fight. My name is Tamaquah, and your battle is my own."

A trick...?

It had to be—what would the *Comanche* know of Tate's fight?

"We have a common enemy." Tamaquah raised his chin. "The ones you call the Bone Orchard Boys."

Tate lowered his aim a fraction, enough to signal his willingness to listen, but not enough to promise the man his next breath.

"Keep talkin'."

"For many winters, these men ride into our hunting grounds, but not to build homes or plant corn." Tamaquah waved one hand to encompass the wide plains stretching beyond the burned ranch. "They burn and kill, they poison the rivers so the buffalo die and leave them to rot under the sun."

The calculating part of Tate, which had helped him survive the war, processed the words. It made sense that the Bone Orchard Boys wouldn't stop their violence at Comanche borders.

Another part of him, however, a fourteen-year-old boy kneeling in the dirt beside his mother's body, screamed that this had to be a *lie*—a carefully crafted story to make him lower his gun.

"We watched them burn your home, saw them ambush you in the snow. That same fire burns our lodges." Tamaquah narrowed his eyes. "Their bullets kill our hunters, and our children go hungry."

A gust of wind tore across the ruin, kicking up a swirl of snowy ashes that stung Tate's eyes. He blinked, and for a second, he saw his father's face in the churning cloud, his jaw set in a stubborn line that Tate now wore as his own.

"Too long have Comanche and white man bled this soil. We can keep spilling blood until the ground drinks us both, or we can fight the *true* wolves together."

Tate sniffed. "And how d'you reckon we do that?"

"We hunt these men down, you and I, and wipe them from this land. Then, when it is done, we can live in peace. Your people on your land, my people on ours."

Peace—a foreign coin from a country Tate had never visited.

He looked around at the skeletal timbers of his home, the scorched earth where Lynda's garden used to grow, and the stark oak where he'd cut her down.

There was no peace here, only a barren monument to everything he'd failed to protect.

He simply couldn't believe it; the Comanche just wanted the gang gone so they could take the land for themselves—the same old story, just with a different beginning. They'd use Tate's grief and guns, and then, when the Bone Orchard Boys had been defeated, they'd turn on him.

He raised the Colt again. "I don't deal with your kind."

"You're making a—"

"You ride onto my land, speaking of peace, but all I hear is the same damn lie my pa heard before you filled his back with arrows. You want this land—that's all you've ever wanted! You just found a new way to ask for it."

Tate's entire body thrummed with the need to pull the trigger, to end this charade and get back to the simple truth of revenge. One bullet was all it would take to make his position clear.

"Tate, hold on." Cade's hand clamped down on his shoulder. "Just hear him out."

"I've heard enough." He tried to shake Cade off, but his grip held fast. "Get *off* me, Cade!"

"No. You ain't thinkin' straight. You're lookin' at him, but you're seein' ghosts from a fight that ended *fourteen years ago.*"

Tate glared at Tamaquah. "You got ten seconds to get your men off my property before I start shootin'."

Cade stepped out from behind the wall and moved between Tate and Tamaquah, holding his Winchester low. "He's got a right to be cautious. We've been burned before."

Tate huffed. "Damn straight, we—"

"We're also trapped, Tate." Cade glanced back. "Storm's on its way, the trail's cold, and the law is useless. We're three guns against a whole damn army. We need to think about this."

Tamaquah inclined his head. "You speak wisdom."

"Give us time to chew on this." Cade tipped his hat. "We'll meet back here two days from now, at sunrise."

Tate's jaw went rigid. Cade had no right to bargain with these devils on *his* land, on the graves of his family. He opened his mouth to shout him down, to tell them all to go to hell, but the words caught in his throat.

If he got himself killed here over old grudges, Marietta would be left to deal with all this alone. Despite his refusal to allow himself to imagine a future with her, he still had to do all in his power to protect her.

"Two days." Tamaquah nodded, then looked at Tate. "Think carefully. A man blinded by old hatred will walk straight into a new fire."

With that, he turned, swung onto his pony, and raised his hand. Without another word, the line of riders wheeled their mounts around and trotted back toward the trees, dissolving into the thickening snow.

Reluctantly, Tate lowered his Colt, then whirled on Cade. "What in the blue blazes were you thinkin'?"

Cade held his hands up as though to calm a spooked horse. "I bought us time, Tate. That's all."

"*Time?*" The word scraped its way from Tate's throat like splintered bone. "You stood on the bones of my family and bargained with the men who put them there! You call that buyin' time?"

"Tate—"

"I call it *treason*."

"Be reasonable."

Tate swept his arm out, taking in the whole doggone graveyard of his life: the skeletal ribs of the barn, the gaping maw of the house, the sentinel oak standing like a hangman's gallows against the bruised purple of the churning sky.

Swirling snow hissed against the charred wood with the melody of whispering specters.

"This is my land, Cade. Mine. You had no right."

"And what right do you have to get us all killed?" Cade crossed his arms. "You were gonna shoot him, weren't you? Just pull that trigger and send us all to hell right along with him!"

"It would've been a better death than what they gave my folks."

"Damn it, Tate, open your eyes!" Cade stepped forward. "That weren't the same man who rode through here fourteen years ago."

"I don't care."

"This ain't the same fight!"

"I don't *care*!"

"We're three men against a phantom who commands an army through that snake of a foreman, Calder, and aims to own this town from the shadows. You wanna fight *that* with three guns and a pocketful of pride?"

Every word struck under Tate's ribs. He knew Cade spoke the cold, miserable logic of truth; the impossible odds stacked against them might well fuel their own funeral pyre. Thing was, the truth of his mind and the truth of his blood spoke two different things—his blood remembered a story written in screams and burning pine.

"I know their kind."

Cade sighed. "Yes, I know what you're—"

"They talk of peace when they want your land. They talk of friendship when they want your guns. A white man and a Comanche can't be friends, Cade, any more than wolves and sheep can share pasture. Sooner or later, the wolf gets hungry."

"That ain't your pa talkin', Tate." Cade shook his head. "That's the scared fourteen-year-old boy who watched him die."

"Cade—"

"I can't blame you for it, Lord knows, but you're lettin' that boy make decisions for the *man* who's gotta fight this war *now*."

Cade was right. But Tate still couldn't bring himself to trust the Comanche. He might as well hand a lit match to a man who'd already doused you in kerosene. The Comanche would point them at the Bone Orchard Boys, goad them into spending their bullets and blood, and when the smoke cleared, the bastards would step over the graves of both sides to claim what was left.

"They're the only help we're like to get." Cade pushed Tate's shoulder. "Grady's got a wife and three kids hidin' in their house, prayin' he don't get himself killed chasin' *your* ghosts."

"I know."

"Fletcher's layin' up in Marietta's guest room with a hole in his side, lookin' over his shoulder for the rest of his days."

"Don't rightly trust him, either."

"And you and me?" Cade snorted. "We got nothin' left to lose except each other, and you seem hell-bent on spendin' that coin, too."

Tate turned away to stare at the ruins. As wind howled through the blackened timbers, he ran a gloved hand over the charred surface of what had once been his home. Soot came away on the leather, a black stain he could never wipe clean.

Cade was right about one thing: they were losing.

They chased shadows, following trails that turned to smoke, and fought an enemy who seemed to know their every move. They huddled over a map in a saloon, drawing circles and lines that meant nothing, while the real power in this county—the ghost in the bandana—sat somewhere warm and laughed at them.

A small voice, one he hadn't heard in years, whispered from a deep and forgotten corner of his mind. It sounded a little like Wyatt—that same practical, no-nonsense tone Tate would hear before a battle: "*What's the plan, Tate? You can't just stand there and get shot.*"

What *was* his plan? Ride into another ambush? Wait for Calder's men to kick in the saloon doors again, this time with enough guns to finish the job?

He'd dragged Marietta and her home squarely in the crosshairs. If pride and old, bitter hatred threatened to drag him under and take *her* with him, he would have to discard it.

For her.

"Two days," he murmured to the burned wood. "We meet him. We listen. That's all."

Cade patted his shoulder. "That's all I'm askin'."

Nodding, Tate looked out at the snow-swept plains—the land his father had bled for, which the Comanche claimed as their own. Wind bit at his face, pelting his skin with ice.

He'd agreed to listen, but... how could they ever truly work together? How could he sit across from a man whose people had brought him so much pain and pretend they were allies?

He'd just betrayed his own dead, trading their memory for a slim chance at survival.

Chapter Sixteen

From her spot behind the bar, Marietta watched the men argue, their words tangling in the smoky air like a knot of fighting snakes.

The groaning blizzard that hammered the saloon walls sounded better than their jawing.

Fletcher slumped in a chair by the hearth. Cade paced the floorboards, thumping a restless rhythm that grated on Marietta's nerves. Grady sat like a mountain, resting his big hands on his knees. Nora, bless her heart, wrung her hands by the stove.

Tate stared out the window.

"This is a fool's errand, I tell you." He tapped the glass with his finger. "Walkin' into their camp, trustin' a man whose kind spit on the ground we walk on. They'll take our guns, spill our blood, and leave our bones for the buzzards when the fight's done."

Lord, give me strength.

Marietta slammed a tin mug onto the bar with a *clang*, making Nora jump. Marietta did *not* need this today. Tate was supposed to be her greatest ally, and she had better things to do than fight his stubborn streak.

"What other choice is there, Tate?" Grady shook his head. "My Sarah-girl asks me every night when the boogeymen are leavin'. You want I tell her we're waitin' on the Good Lord to ride down and do it for us?"

"Grady's got the right of it." Cade stopped pacing and planted his hands on the table. "We've been spinnin' our wheels for weeks."

When Tate turned from the window, the look in his dark eyes could have frozen fire. "I know their kind. They'll smile to your face and stick a knife in your back."

There it is.

The root of it all, watered with silence and cultivated in darkness, had nothing to do with tactics or the risk of a shaky alliance. No, this came from a deeper wound Tate refused to show anyone, even as it bled all over everything he touched.

Marietta pushed off the bar and walked to the table. Planting her palms on the scarred oak, she leaned her full weight on it. Everyone looked at her, but she kept her eyes on Tate.

"So we just sit on our hands?"

"Marietta—"

"We sit here, snowed in, and wait for 'em to kick in our door again? Wait for 'em to finish the job they started with my uncle? Your spread? Cade's family?"

"This ain't about doin' nothin', Marietta, it's about not gettin' ourselves planted six feet under for a promise that ain't worth spit."

"That's a wager I'm willin' to make." She straightened, crossing her arms over her chest. "The other choice is sittin' here like fattened calves, waitin' for the slaughter. We got a name: Ransom Calder. We got a foe in common with a man who knows these hills like the back of his hand. That's a sight more than we had yesterday."

Tate stepped away from the window and moved into the circle of light. The lines around his mouth carved deep into his skin, and a muscle jumped in his jaw.

"You don't understand," he said. "This is about more than just revenge."

A hot spike shot through Marietta, nearly stealing her breath. How could he stand there, after all they'd shared—the quiet talks and almost-kiss branded on her memory—and act like she was some naive schoolgirl?

"Don't you dare," she whispered, her voice shaking with a fury that surprised even her. "Don't you *dare* stand there and preach to me like I don't understand the stakes."

"I know you do, but—"

"My uncle is cold in the ground. His blood stained these very floorboards. The man who gave that order is still out there, breathing air that my uncle *can't*. That's all the understanding I need!"

"See?" He jabbed a finger in her direction. "That's what this is for you: a necktie party. You want blood, and you don't care who helps you get it. But some lines, a man of honor don't cross."

Honor.

He'd hurled the word at her like a rock, a word for men who had the luxury of choice, who weren't fighting for their very survival. The unfairness of it, the sheer *hypocrisy*, clawed up her throat.

"You want to talk about *honor*? You, who came to my door, bleeding, for us to patch you up, feed you, and put a roof over your head?"

He flinched.

"You're a *liar*, Tate Hollister, hidin' behind high-and-mighty talk when you *know* this is our only play. You know Grady's right, Cade's right, and *I'm* right. But you won't do it."

She took a step closer, right into his space, forcing him to meet her eyes.

"You're a *coward*."

"*What?*"

"You ain't scared they'll turn on us. No, you're scared to stand on that patch of burned earth and face the ghosts you been runnin' from—to look a Comanche in the eye and see a *man* lookin' back instead of a monster, 'cause if you do, your whole story turns to dust—and what'll you be then?"

A sound tore from his throat, a mix of a growl and a scream, and he swept his arm across the nearest table. Mugs and cards flew through the air, crashing to the floor with a clatter of tin and a flutter of paper.

"You know *nothing!*"

He turned, snatched up his coat, and stormed toward the door. As he wrenched it open, an icy vortex roared into the room, extinguishing lamps and sending a deep chill through the saloon. Then, he vanished into the white fury, slamming the door shut behind him.

Marietta trembled like a trapped bird as she stared at the door, half-expecting him to burst right back through it.

"I, uh..." Nora pulled her shawl tight around her shoulders. "I oughtta see to our inventory."

Then, she gave Marietta a look filled with pity Marietta did *not* want, and scurried out the back way.

Grady rose to his feet next, blocking what little light emanated from the remaining lamp with his great frame.

"My wife will be wonderin' what's takin' so long." He clasped the back of a chair. "Tate'll come around, Marietta. His bark's worse than his bite."

With a solemn nod, he followed Nora out into the storm.

Cade righted the overturned table, then cleared his throat. "Hell of a thing to say."

"He had it coming."

"Maybe," he allowed as he stacked the cards into a neat pile, "but you stuck a knife in the one place he ain't got no armor."

"What's your point?"

He finally looked at her. "He just needs time. You threw his whole world sideways, askin' him to do this. He's got half a lifetime of hate built up like a stone wall inside him. A man can't tear down a wall like that in one night."

"We don't *have* time, Cade."

"He'll come around."

"I don't think he will."

"When the time comes, he'll do what's right. Not for his own sake, but for you—for all of us. He just..." Cade sighed. "He's gotta face his own demons first, and you just handed 'em a whole new set of swords."

Cade put the cards on the bar, grabbed his coat, and tipped his hat. Then, he left, leaving her alone in the vast saloon, deep shadows pooling in every corner and crevice.

Ain't even courtin' yet, and we already had a fight.

She'd seen Tate's moods, his silences, and the darkness that pulled at him, but never such raw and uncontrolled rage. She had put it there, taken his deepest pain, and used it as a weapon against him.

A bitter taste filled her mouth.

Was this what vengeance had made of her? A woman who'd gut a man with words just to win an argument?

She sank into the chair Tate had vacated and buried her face in her hands. The wood still held a faint warmth from his body.

Or, maybe, she just imagined it.

***

As night fell, the blizzard reached its full fury. Snow piled high against the doors, and the wind screamed like a banshee.

Marietta sat by the hearth, the shotgun resting across her lap, and watched the embers glow. Every *creak* of settling wood made her jump, though Fletcher's snores from upstairs provided some semblance of normalcy.

Behind the bar, the door leading to the kitchen and storeroom rattled.

Instinctively, she lifted the shotgun, but the splintering *crash* of an attack failed to come. Instead, the latch shuddered, and the door creaked open to admit a figure, which slouched in like a criminal caught red-handed in the act.

Tate pushed the door shut, sealing it against the storm's fury, and slid the bolt home. For a long moment, he just stood there, his shoulders slumped and chest heaving.

Marietta lowered the shotgun.

Slowly, Tate ambled into the main room, shedding clumps of snow with every step, and stopped a few feet from her. His dark eyes found hers in the dim light.

"I'm sorry."

She raised an eyebrow.

"What you said..." He ran a hand through his damp hair. "You were right. All of it. Standin' on my land, seeing them there... it brought it all back. The smell of smoke. My ma... It was too much."

"I know."

He looked away from her and toward the embers. "But that ain't no excuse. I had no right to talk to you that way. To throw your grief back in your face."

"No. You didn't."

He finally met her eyes again. "You're right. It's the only way. We got to work with them."

She sighed. "Tate—"

"I'll be movin' out soon, anyway."

Marietta swallowed her half-formed apology.

"Need to get back to the ranch. Barn's mostly gone, but the foundation is still sound. I'll build somethin' small on it—a line cabin—enough to keep the snow out. Reckon I can be out of your hair in a few days."

"That's it?" She jumped up and stormed over to him. "One disagreement, and you want to *leave*? After everything? After we almost..."

She closed her eyes and took a deep breath.

"Yes." He shook his head. "I'll understand if you hate me after tonight."

Buildin' them walls right back up.

Just when she'd thought they'd moved beyond that, when they should be mending things between them, he was pulling back again—as if he could just come here, apologize, and agree with her, then leave immediately. Like she'd let him push her away before she could get any closer.

No. Not this time.

"You, Tate Hollister, are damn fool." She jabbed her index finger into his chest. "A stubborn, pigheaded fool!"

Before he could react, before he could put up another wall of words, she grabbed the front of his damp coat with both hands, pulled him down to her, and pressed her mouth to his.

Chapter Seventeen

Two days dragged past like a gut-shot man crawling for cover, and each minute scraped Tate raw. The blizzard had finally descended upon the world in full. Arriving with a slow hiss, it erased the surface of the land until only a roiling maelstrom of alabaster remained.

Beneath Tate's boots, the ground of his own spread protested with a deep and mournful groan. Snow piled against the blackened bones of the cabin and filled the empty sockets where glass had once been.

A man could stand here and never know a house had ever existed, but Tate remembered every nail he'd driven, each plank he'd set, and the memory left a taste like ash and rust on his tongue.

Cade stood a few feet away, Winchester in hand. Grady planted his feet and pulled his collar tight around his neck, his breath pluming like smoke from a dying fire.

Fletcher looked more like a spooked coyote than a man and shifted his weight from foot to foot near the ruin of the barn. Even so, Tate had to give credit where credit was due: Nora's skill was to be commended.

After this meeting, Fletcher would head for some trapper's line cabin he'd found to hole up and lick his wounds. Tate didn't envy him the journey; no man should travel alone in a storm like this one.

Then, there was Marietta, standing her ground against the gale. Wind whipped dark curls across her face and plastered her coat against her frame.

He tried not to look at her, but his eyes betrayed him, seeking her out against the swirling white.

Two nights ago, she'd kissed him; it hadn't been a gentle thing, either. No, she'd pulled him down and branded him. Her mouth had spoken a language his body understood, even if his mind refused to translate it.

For a moment, the ice in his veins had cracked as warmth flooded the hollow in his chest. Then, the ghosts had screamed, and he'd pulled away. Again.

They hadn't spoken of it. Not a word.

He told himself she regretted it. That, in a moment of grief and fury, she'd just been groping desperately for another soul in the dark.

How long you gonna lie to yourself, Hollister?

He kicked at a shard of frozen mud.

She came to stand beside him. "You're wound tighter than a fiddle string."

He kept his eyes on the tree line. "Just want to get this over with."

Her gloved hand touched his arm briefly, a faint pressure that barely registered through the thick wool of his coat, but a jolt shot through him all the same. He fought the urge to cover her hand with his own, to hold on to that small point of warmth. Instead, he forced his muscles to unclench and his jaw to loosen.

She pulled her hand away. "They'll come."

He hated this. Standing over the tomb where his past lay buried with the people who symbolized his broken present, waiting to bargain with the very specters of his nightmares.

Cade had been right; Tate *had* let the frightened boy from his past decide his future for too long. That boy still screamed inside him, yet he had to do this. Not for himself—he had nothing worth saving—but for Marietta, for Grady's family, and the whole damn town she cared so much about.

He owed her that much.

Just as last time, the Comanche announced themselves with a low thrum that rose into drumming beneath the frozen ground. Then, they emerged from the blizzard like spirits conjured from the storm itself. One moment, a colorless curtain flailed before them; the next, dark shapes materialized on lean ponies.

Tate clasped the grip of his Colt.

Cade stepped up beside him. "I can take the lead on this, Tate. If you want."

Tate tore his eyes from the approaching riders and looked at Cade.

A year ago, he might've accepted. Might've stepped back and let Cade do the talking while he stood guard with his thumb on the hammer. But things had changed. *He* had changed. With Marietta's eyes on his back, he couldn't act like the coward she'd accused him of being.

He shook his head. "I got it."

Tamaquah approached alone and, as before, stopped a dozen yards away. This time, he didn't dismount, but he raised his empty palms again.

"You came."

"We came to listen."

"I will tell you again, so there's no confusion. My people suffer." Tamaquah's gaze swept over their small group, lingering briefly on Marietta before returning to Tate. "The men you hunt, who leave bone orchards in their wake, want the land—and not to live on or grow things."

"To sell, I know."

"You do *not* know." Tamaquah frowned. "Your face tells me you resent us for wanting our land back."

Tate clenched his jaw. "I resent fightin' over it."

"This land has been ours since the stars were young." Tamaquah sighed. "We get nowhere arguing over it now. Let us deal with these black-hearted men first."

"What can you tell us of them?" Tate raised his chin. "Do you know who leads them?"

"We only met his right hand, the man called Ransom Calder." Tamaquah inhaled. "He offered guns and whiskey to drive the white ranchers from their homes. He said, when it was done, the land would be ours again."

Grady let out a low growl. "The sons of guns tried to set us against each other."

Cade tilted his head. "Obviously, you didn't take the offer."

"They seek to burn the whole prairie." Tamaquah shook his head. "We told him to take his poison back to his master. Ever since, his men have hunted us in the night. They do not fight like warriors, face to face, but shoot from the trees. They kill our women when they gather wood. They are *cowards*."

The story had the ring of truth—the miserable, dirty truth that men lived and died by out here. Fletcher hadn't lied; the conspiracy did indeed stretch far beyond what Tate could have imagined. This wasn't about a few scattered ranches.

It was about the entire territory.

Still, even now, he needed more—some kind of assurance that the Comanche wouldn't stab them in the back. It had gnawed at him for two days and kept him staring at the ceiling in the dead of night.

"We heard your story, and it lines up with what we know." Tate took a deep breath. "But words are wind, Tamaquah. How do we trust you?"

"We will not betray you."

"Maybe not while we fight together, but when Calder and his boss are in the ground, what then? How can we be sure you won't turn on us and finish the job they started?"

Tamaquah held his gaze as the blizzard shrieked around them.

Tate considered himself a good judge of character, and he saw no guile on the face of the man in front of him, no cunning of a wolf waiting for the sheep to lower its guard—only the same weary resolve Tate saw in his own reflection.

The Comanche had been pushed to the brink, and Tamaquah was here to fight for the survival of his people.

"When I was a boy, my father taught me that a man's word is the stone upon which he builds his lodge." Tamaquah dismounted. "If the stone is weak, the lodge will fall."

Tate took a step closer and smiled. "My pa used to say something similar."

"My word is stone, Tate Hollister. We fight this enemy together, and when the last of their kind is gone from this land, we *will* have peace. The blood that has soaked this ground for generations will finally have a chance to dry."

Then, Tamaquah reached into a leather pouch at his side and pulled out something that glinted in the gray light. He tossed it through the air, and it landed in the snow at Tate's feet.

Tate bent down and picked it up. It was a sheriff's badge, but it was tarnished and bent, with a dark stain marring its surface.

"We found one of their camps a moon ago," Tamaquah said. "They had killed a lawman from the next county over, a man who got too close. They are not mere outlaws, but a sickness that rots flesh—and rot must be cut out, lest it kill the whole body."

Tate closed his hand around the badge.

With the metal cooling his palm, he looked from the badge to Tamaquah, then Cade and Grady, and finally, to Marietta. For better or worse, he had his answer: he had to trust Tamaquah.

There was no other way.

Before he could offer his word to the Comanche, however, a high, thin cry cut through the storm. Though the wind tore it away quickly, Tate would've recognized that sound anywhere.

A horse's neigh.

It came from the west, deep within the swirling chaos of the blizzard.

Tamaquah's head snapped in the direction of the sound. "Those are not my men."

Tate dropped the badge and drew his Colt.

Beside him, Cade and Grady raised their rifles as Fletcher scrambled for cover behind the burned-out chimney. Marietta worked the lever on her Winchester with a clanking *shuck-shuck*.

The Comanche warriors drew their bows.

The snow distorted, blurring shapes and warping sound. Somewhere in that white void, another horse whinnied, but farther away this time.

Looks like they decided not to come after us.

Tate didn't blame them. With so many Comanche around and Tate's group hiding behind cover, it would be the height of foolishness to launch an attack now. Still, the outlaws—Tate was certain it had been them—had left their message.

They'd seen everything.

Chapter Eighteen

One day had passed since they stood on the frozen bones of Tate's ranch, and the world had spent it dissolving into white fury.

Marietta had barely found a spare minute to draw a full breath, let alone sift through what had happened out there in the snow. The blizzard had driven every man who wasn't a trapper—or a fool—indoors, swelling the saloon with bodies and noise.

The room was packed from wall to wall, and the resulting din rattled the bottles behind the bar. She'd been working from dawn until the lamps had been lit. Her arms ached, and her ears rang from the constant racket.

Despite the commotion, her mind drifted back to the storm.

It wasn't the blizzard that worried her, but the presence within—the neigh that had sliced through the howling wind to hang in the air like an icy question mark.

Someone had been watching them.

The realization sat in her belly like a cold stone with a certainty that defied logic, yet held fast all the same. Their small band of ghosts and fighters had stood on that burned-out patch of land as unseen eyes measured them from the trees.

The saloon grew thick with sweat, spilled whiskey, and the stench of men who knew fear but refused to name it. She moved through the chaos, keeping her feet sure and her hands working. A nod here, a poured drink there, a quick wipe to erase the wet rings on the bar.

Her body knew this dance, but her mind had wandered miles away, to Tate—the ghost of his warmth, his phantom hand on her arm, and the unsettling silence between them after her reckless kiss.

She'd thrown a stone into the deep well of his grief, and she still waited to hear it hit the bottom.

Suddenly, the saloon doors crashed open, smacking against the inside walls. The blizzard roared in, flowing around a figure filling the doorway to assault the room's occupants, guttering half the lamps on the far wall. Cards flew from a table, scattering like dead leaves, eliciting a collective groan of outrage.

Marietta's hand went to her shotgun. "You aim to freeze us all to death? Close the damn door!"

The figure stumbled forward and pushed the doors shut. The screaming wind receded, leaving the comparatively calm commotion to fill the saloon again. The man stamped snow from his boots and pushed back the brim of his hat.

Light from the remaining lamps revealed the face of Amos Sharpe.

Men shifted nervously, dropping their voices to low mutters.

What's the sheriff doing here?

Walker Saloon was not a place for a man who polished his star more than he cleaned his gun. Uncle Everett had paid his dues—enough to keep the law looking the other way when a card game got too rowdy or a brawl spilled into the street—but the sheriff himself had stayed away.

So why in God's good name had he come *now*, through the heart of a blizzard, into a room of men who saw his badge as a target?

"You dirty son of a gun!" Jedediah, his face flushed with cheap whiskey, threw his chair back. "You palmed that card! I saw you!"

Silas stood slowly. "You're drunk, Jed. Go sleep it off before you do somethin' you'll regret."

Marietta frowned.

Didn't they have this exact same conversation last time?

"The only thing I regret is not knockin' your teeth down your throat the last time you cheated me!"

No. Just... *no.* Not tonight. They could stay away from the same tired song and dance for one blasted night.

Taking the shotgun with her, Marietta moved from behind the bar. "That's enough, Jedediah. I'll brook no trouble here tonight."

Jedediah lunged across the table, and Silas met him with a roar. They crashed together in a clumsy tangle of limbs, then slammed against a support post, grunting and cursing, skidding on the sawdust-covered floor.

The others backed away, forming a loose circle.

They wanted a show—always did—to watch the blood fly and feel the thrill of a fight they were too scared to start themselves.

Cowards.

However, just as Marietta stepped forward to knock some sense into them, Sharpe pushed through the circle of men with quiet authority that left Marietta honestly shocked. Then, he grabbed the scrappers by their collars and, with surprising strength, tore them apart, then threw them in opposite directions.

Jedediah and Silas gaped at the polished star on his chest.

"This here saloon's closed for the night." Sheriff Sharpe looked at everyone in the room. "Goodnight."

Grumbling rose from the crowd, but no one argued.

Marietta couldn't blame them. The fight was over, and the presence of the law—even a lazy sheriff like Sharpe, who never seemed to do anything—must've soured their whiskey. One by one, they shuffled toward the door, pulling on coats and grabbing hats, darting glances at the sheriff and Marietta.

Sheriff Sharpe held Jedediah and Silas pinned with his glare until everyone else had left. Then, he shoved them toward the door.

"If I see either of you again before morning, you'll be sleeping it off in a cell."

They stumbled out into the storm without a backward glance; the door swung shut behind them, leaving the vast, empty room in silence. The litter of overturned chairs, papers, and tables did little to counter the void that now crept in to gnaw at Marietta.

She let out a slow breath. "I appreciate the help, Sheriff. I could have handled it, but—"

"No need to thank me." He walked to a table and began righting the chairs. "A town gets coiled up tight in a storm like this. Sometimes, it needs a firm hand to keep from strangling itself."

Then, he sat down at the table in the corner—right where Uncle Everett used to sit—and took off his hat.

"Pour me a whiskey, would you?" He ran a hand through his sandy hair. "The good stuff." He chuckled. "Reckon I've earned it."

Marietta hesitated for a moment, then went behind the bar to retrieve a bottle of bourbon and a clean glass. She poured a generous measure and carried it to his table, then crossed her arms.

He took a slow sip. "Busy night."

"The blizzard keeps 'em in."

"It does." He stared into the amber liquid in his glass. "How goes the search for your uncle's killer? You and Hollister makin' any headway?"

Marietta's spine went rigid. She and the others had agreed: not a word about the Comanche. Not to anyone. The town had too many ears, and they didn't know which ones listened for the ghost in the bandana. Useless as he was, the sheriff might let something slip and ruin them all.

"It's a fool's errand, Sheriff." She shrugged and heaved an exaggerated sigh, doing her best to sound defeated. "We've been chasing shadows down a trail cold as frost under snow. It's like whoever leads 'em don't even exist, 'cept as a whisper. A ghost."

"Perhaps," he drawled, swirling the whiskey in his glass, "that's for the best."

"What's that supposed to mean?"

He looked up at her then. "Marietta, you're a respectable woman, running a business on your own. It's a hard thing. Ain't rightly smart to go kickin' a hornet's nest you can't see."

Ice crept through her bones.

"My uncle is dead, Sheriff." She frowned. "Them hornets already got their stingers out."

"I understand your grief—I truly do—but some outlaws are more dangerous than others." He took another sip of his whiskey. "They're a different breed. They don't just take your property. They'll burn your world down around you and enjoy the warmth of the blaze. You have no idea what kind of man you're messing with."

What...?

This ominous talk didn't sound like anything she'd ever heard come out of Sheriff Sharpe's mouth; words like this belonged on the lips of lawmen who actually went out and *did* their jobs. What could Sharpe possibly have learned about the man in the bandana from the comfort of his office?

"Understand what I'm sayin'?"

"Can't say I do, Sheriff."

"In simple terms, this town has seen enough bloodshed." He stroked the star on his chest with a smooth thumb. "I won't have more on my hands because a grieving niece decides to play lawman."

She glowered at him.

He thought she was *playing*? If he'd done his job—or any *portion* of it—she'd be free to run her saloon and mourn her uncle in peace! Still... little good could come from unleashing her tongue on him now, making an enemy out of him. A useless, yet friendly, lawman was a thousand times better than an enemy with a badge who held a grudge.

She pressed her lips into a thin line. "I still don't get your meaning, Sheriff."

Sharpe sighed. "Let me be *perfectly* clear: you and your friends need to stay *out* of it. Leave it to me. It's for your own good."

She nodded slowly. "If you say so..."

He finished his whiskey, setting the glass on the table with a *click*. Standing up, he put on his hat and tugged the brim down.

"Have a good night, Marietta. Bolt your door."

He walked to the door and let himself out, vanishing into the storm as quickly as he'd appeared.

Marietta stared at the door long after he'd gone out.

That—all of it—had been so jarringly out of character that it wasn't even funny. His sudden competence and strength, the strange warning... What was the sheriff's game? Genuine words of caution from a lazy lawman who knew he was in over his head? A concerned man trying to protect a woman he saw as vulnerable?

Or was it something else?

She replayed his words in her mind.

"You have no idea what kind of man you're messing with."

That didn't sound like speculation, but a statement of fact—a man describing a wolf he'd seen up close.

One he knows by name.

Marietta almost discarded the insane thought as soon as it crossed her mind, but... What if Sharpe was somehow connected to the Bone Orchard Boys? Could *he* be the informant feeding the bandana man all he needed to know?

Stay out of it.

As menacing as Sharpe's warning had felt, it *could* still have been genuine concern, even if it had the feel of a threat.

Problem was, it could've been either.

Or worse, both.

Chapter Nineteen

From the back of his gelding, Tate watched Tamaquah's shoulders move with the rhythm of his pony against a churning boil of white and gray. A man could get lost and freeze to death ten feet from his own front door in this squall.

A fool's errand.

When Tate had insisted that he and the Comanche go alone, Cade and Grady had argued against it, saying that riding into a blizzard on a ghost hunt with only two men was a fine way to get yourself killed. Tate, of course, had turned the argument around on them, selling it as a matter of caution, a way to keep the others safe from the storm's teeth—four were just as likely to kick the bucket as two, after all.

He hadn't said it aloud, but as always, it was about making sure Grady survived to go home to his family.

On the other hand, Tate absolutely could've taken Cade, but Cade had a way of seeing—and constantly talking about—things Tate would rather keep buried as deep as he could shove them.

And so, he had ridden into this bleached hell, which swallowed all sight and sound, with a man whose silence fell heavier than a tombstone. Tate had to give Tamaquah credit: he rode as if the storm were no more than a gentle rain. His tough little buckskin pony seemed to navigate by feel alone, picking through the deepening drifts without a moment's hesitation.

"They ain't fools, you know." Tate ducked under a low pine branch. "Won't keep to one spot. Gang like that got a dozen bolt-holes."

Inevitably, Tamaquah replied with logical simplicity that, while maddening, Tate had grown to admire—if grudgingly.

"Even the wolf must return to its den."

If this were any other outlaw band, Tate might have agreed—a pack of bandits *would* need a place to count coin and drink whiskey—but he suspected the Bone Orchard Boys' leader was too smart for that. He'd keep his men on the move, slinking into a den with each season, never letting complacency become a liability.

Tate scanned the trees; each snow-laden branch and dark shadow in the shrubbery could hide an ambush. He'd led his friends into one trap already; he wasn't eager to ride into another.

"They'll see us comin' a mile off."

"The storm is a shield to blind the eye and muffle the ear."

I'm a damn fool.

Again, Tate wondered if he was crazy to trust this man and risk the storm, thinking this fool's errand would accomplish anything at all.

Then, Tamaquah pointed a gloved finger at the thick carpet of snow. "A heavy man rode a horse with iron shoes through here."

How on God's green earth did he see that?

Tate swung down from his gelding and crouched, seeing the faint depression where Tamaquah had pointed: the faint outline of a horseshoe. Comanche ponies went unshod—which meant a white man's mount had left this print.

Tate straightened and brushed snow from his pants. "One track don't make a trail."

"No." Tamaquah stood and swept his gaze through the woods, seeming to miss nothing. "But it speaks. This man was not hunting. He rode with purpose. He did not linger."

Tamaquah urged his pony deeper into the timber, so Tate mounted his gelding and followed.

Tate watched Tamaquah's back, his posture, how he held his head, reading the broken twigs and disturbed snow like a preacher reading from the Good Book.

Ain't no outlaw gun as menacing as a competent tracker.

Though a portion of Tate's unease came from his lingering mistrust of the Comanche, more pertinently, skilled trackers like Tamaquah tended to trust their instincts without question—a trait that often led men into traps.

Nothin' for it but to keep going.

They stopped only to rest the horses. Time lost meaning as the sun formed a pale smudge somewhere behind the curtain of the storm. They rode until Tate's thighs ached from gripping the saddle, the cold sinking so deep into his bones, he wondered if he'd ever feel warm again.

Finally, as they huddled in the lee of a granite outcropping to let the horses breathe, Tamaquah found the second sign: a spot of missing bark, high on the trunk of an old pine— too high for deer, but just the height of a man's shoulder on horseback.

Wordlessly, Tamaquah touched the graze, came away with something pinched between his thumb and forefinger, and handed it to Tate.

Tate squinted at the tiny fiber in his palm: a thread of coarse, cheap wool, like a saddle tramp—or outlaw—might wear. As much as Tate hated to admit it, it looked like Tamaquah had been right.

Seems like we're closin' in.

They pushed on, the gently rolling plains giving way to steeper country. Wind threatened to shove both horse and rider from the track as they entered a rugged land of canyons and sharp ridges.

Eventually, Tamaquah pulled his pony to a halt at the edge of a long, U-shaped ravine. "There," he said, pointing to the far side of the chasm, where trees grew thick and dark. "They will make their camp where the wind cannot bite. A place with water that a man can defend."

Tate followed his finger, peering through the swirling snow, but could only see a wall of white and the dark shapes of pines beyond. Even so, he didn't reject the possibility immediately—the signs had led to this godforsaken slash in the earth, after all—so the den was likely *somewhere* around here.

Tamaquah led his pony along the rim of the ravine, and Tate followed.

"Tate Hollister." Tamaquah turned in his saddle and looked at Tate. "I would ask you a question."

Tate shrugged. "Shoot."

"Why does your heart carry such hate for my people?"

Tate worked his jaw, feeling the muscles bunch under his skin, and kept his eyes on the gray swirl ahead. He could tell Tamaquah to go to hell, spur his horse, and leave the Comanche standing there, all alone. He could've done a hundred things other than respond to a question that *had* no good answer.

"I don't waste good breath on feelings," he rasped. "A man keeps his eyes on a rattler, but that don't mean he holds a grudge against it—just that he knows what it is."

"And you know what my people are?"

"I know the color of the blood they spill." Tate reined his gelding to a halt and turned in the saddle to face Tamaquah. "I learned at Shiloh, and Chickamauga, and a hundred other mud-soaked patches of hell."

Tamaquah stopped beside Tate. "I do not deny that the river of blood between us flows deep and runs red."

"Damn right, it does."

"Sometimes, a great fire burns on *both* banks of that river. A man must decide if he will cross the water to fight the flames, or if he will stand alone and let the fire consume him."

Ain't that a good way to put it?

Fire had consumed Tate's whole world.

"I was fourteen."

What in the hell am I doing?

"My folks had a small spread, not far from here."

Why am I saying this?

He'd never shared the grisly details—not with Cade or Grady, or even Lynda—the wound lay too deep. Maybe the storm had pulled it out, this world of white noise that swallowed everything but the man in front of him, or it might've been Tamaquah's steady gaze, which held no judgment, only a deep and weary knowing.

Maybe I'm just tired of carrying the weight.

"They were good people. Prayed every night. Pa worked the land until his hands bled. Ma... she sang while she worked." Tate looked down. "My baby sister, Sarah, weren't more than a year old."

Staring into the middle distance, Tate could almost see the burned ruins of his home, and the rest of the story blurred together. One word at a time, the tale spewed out like black tar, leaving fire and sickness simmering in his gut.

Once he'd finished, he looked back at Tamaquah. "That's why I don't trust your kind. A boy learns a lesson like that, he don't ever forget it."

"I mourn the loss of your family, Tate Hollister, and I share your pain." Tamaquah's exhale joined the moan of the wind. "White men took my father from this world."

Tate raised his eyebrows. "What?"

"They came in the night with fire and rifles, saying he'd stolen a cow. My father was a hunter, not a thief, but they did not listen. They left him in the dirt for the jackal."

Tate huffed. He'd expected denial, an excuse, an argument that his family had somehow deserved their fate. Not *this*. Not a shared piece of jagged history. Yet, now that he'd heard the other side of the story, he couldn't *unhear* it.

Maybe the line between us ain't that thick after all.

The sickness in this land, which pitted man against man over dirt and grass, stretched back farther than he could see: generation after generation of sons burying fathers.

Tate clenched his reins. "Reckon this fight is older than both of us."

Tamaquah nodded. "And it will outlive us—but this enemy we hunt now, these Bone Orchard Boys... They are different."

He frowned. "They do not fight for land to *live* on. They do not fight for honor or for their people, but for coin, poisoning the ground for gold. Their plague will kill us *all* if we let it."

Crack

Crack-Crack

Three gunshots boomed through the storm's howl, one after another.

Tate grabbed his Colt. "The gang?"

"A hunter does not fire three shots so fast at a deer in this storm."

Damn it.

This trip was supposed to be about reconnaissance: find the gang, learn their patterns, plan an ambush. Now, they'd stumbled upon something more, but that didn't change their objective.

Doggone fool's errand just turned into a suicide mission.

"We'll continue on foot." Tate swung down from his gelding. "Quieter that way."

Tamaquah dismounted and pulled a long-barreled rifle from the scabbard on his pony.

They tied their mounts in a thicket of young pines, where heavy branches offered some cover from snow and prying eyes. Tate checked the action on his Colt and pulled his Henry rifle from his saddle. Then, he and Tamaquah moved out, melting into the trees along the ravine's edge.

Planting his feet carefully to avoid dry twigs and loose stones, Tate kept low, using trees for cover. Beside him, Tamaquah slithered like an otherworldly specter, pointing out signs Tate would've missed otherwise: scuff marks on tree bark, a disturbed patch of snow.

As they crept around the edge of the ravine, passing a box canyon formed by the U-curve, and closed in on the other side, the scent of smoke reached Tate on the wind—evidence of men who burned wood without care for who might find them.

Tamaquah dropped to his belly, and Tate followed suit. They crawled through the pines—which really *were* much thicker on this side—until they saw a clearing in the distance.

There, sheltered from the worst of the wind, a camp sprawled in the snow.

Found you.

A large bonfire roared inside a ring of stones, spitting sparks into the swirling flakes. Its light painted half a dozen rough tents in shades of red and orange, their canvas sides flapping with every gust that swirled up from the canyon. At least fifteen horses stood tethered in a makeshift corral at the far end of the camp.

Men moved in the firelight: one turned a spitted deer carcass over the flames, its skin crackling as fat dripped to hiss in the flames; another sharpened a long knife on a whetstone; still others huddled in a group, passing a bottle between them.

Tate glowered.

They look comfortable. Eight, nine, ten of them.

"Tate." Tamaquah shifted and pointed at a tall, wiry figure stepping out of the largest tent. "See that man?"

All sharp angles on a thin frame, this man wore a dark coat, much finer than any of the others Tate could see, and a wide-brimmed black Stetson on his head.

"What about him?"

"*That* is Ransom Calder."

Chapter Twenty

"Beau!" Ransom hollered toward one of the tents. "Get our guest out here!"

Tate flattened his belly against the frozen earth, the icy crust atop the snow groaning softly as it cracked beneath him. Judging by the faint *shhh* of shifting hides beside him, Tamaquah was watching just as intently.

In the clearing, erratic firelight painted the swirling snow in jagged strokes of copper and pitch. Men moved in the open, believing the storm provided a steel wall to hide behind.

Fools. The storm hides the hunter, same as the prey.

A younger man scrambled out from the largest tent, stumbling slightly, his head ducked low.

This must be Beau.

Although he was lean, with a boy's lack of heft, he took time to scan the camp instead, then ducked back under the canvas flap. A moment later, he reappeared, dragging someone behind him by a rope around the wrists.

The captive stumbled, his feet caught in the churned, muddy slush near the fire. A coarse burlap sack—the kind used for grain or potatoes—covered his head, bunching around his shoulders. The heavy buffalo coat, which nearly swallowed his relatively small frame, tugged at a thread of memory in Tate's mind.

I've seen that coat before...

Beau shoved the captive forward, and he hit the ground hard, sprawling to his knees a few feet from Ransom. He let out a grunt, which the thick sack muffled into a low wheeze.

Ransom took a slow step forward, his long coat open to show a matched pair of Colts on his hips. He looked down at the kneeling figure without blinking or frowning; he just tilted his head and watched the man shiver.

"Well, well… Look what the cat dragged in." Ransom's voice slithered through the air like oiled leather, raising the hair on the back of Tate's neck. "Or what my dogs ran to ground, I suppose. Tell me, how's that hole in your side?"

Tate's stomach turned over. Breath caught and burned in his lungs. Tate had been shot in his side, and Nora had stitched up a similar 'hole' on Fletcher's side.

But Fletcher is safe in the saloon… right?

Beau laughed. "This'un ain't much for talkin', Ransom. Maybe we oughtta loosen his tongue?" Not waiting for an answer, he stepped forward and swung his boot into the captive's ribs.

The man let out a strangled cry and toppled onto his side, curling his knees to his chest.

"Now, now, Beau…" The corner of Ransom's mouth twitched upward. "Don't break our new toy too quickly."

Smirking, Beau raised his hands in mock surrender.

"We had a deal, you and I." Ransom nudged the man with the toe of his boot, barely lifting his leg, as if he were moving a pile of horse dung off the path. "I shoot you, and you have the good sense to lie down and *die*. But you—you just *had* to be stubborn and go crawlin' back to town, didn't you?"

Tate's grip tightened on his Colt until the freezing metal bit his palm. His side throbbed with the ghost of the bullet that had put him in the dirt. He remembered the grit under his fingernails as he crawled, a red smear melting the snow beneath him.

Fletcher made that same trip.

Now, this poor man—and Tate couldn't think of who else it could be *but* Fletcher—had found himself back in the grip of the same devils who'd almost killed him.

Tate's mind replayed the last two days: the ride back from his ranch, the arguments in the saloon, and the moment the blizzard had sealed them in. Fletcher had been there, slumped by the fire.

Did he leave at some point?

He tried to picture it, but all he could see was Marietta.

The taste of her sweet breath and the heat of her skin against his formed a fog in his head thicker than the snow. Thinking back to after he'd kissed her, he tried to see past her face and remember if anyone had walked out the door while he was drowning in the scent of her hair, but the image wouldn't come.

Did I let a man walk to his grave because I was too busy looking at a woman's mouth?

Beau hauled the captive back to his knees. "Boss wants to know who you talked to. The saloon gal? That broken-down rancher she's keepin'?"

The captive shook his head so hard that the burlap sack whipped back and forth, snapping against his shoulders.

Ransom exhaled noisily and slumped his shoulders. "Y'see, this is what I don't understand. We had you dead to rights, left you for the coyotes—a clean, simple end."

Beau shook the man again. "Sure was."

"Yet, not only are you still breathin', you *still* won't cooperate." Ransom crouched next to the man. "If I'd known you were tough enough to survive a bullet *and* a blizzard, I would've taken the time to bury you proper—maybe while you were still kickin'."

He drew back and slapped the man through the burlap with a *crack* that echoed through the quiet camp.

The captive snapped to the side and would've fallen again, but Beau held him up by his coat's thick, shaggy collar.

Tate's jaw locked so hard that his teeth ached. Blood rushed into his ears, drowning out the wind.

If this was Fletcher—and it *had* to be—Tate's own blindness had delivered him right back into the enemy's clutches. First, he'd lost his family, then Wyatt, then Lynda... and now, *this*.

Everything I touch, everyone I try to protect, ends up broken or in the ground.

"You know, I almost *admire* your grit." Ransom stood and circled the kneeling man. "Draggin' yourself all the way back to town to find your friends. Must've felt real safe sittin' by their fire, thinkin' you'd cheated the devil."

Beau spat on the ground. "Stupid cur."

"But the devil always collects his due." Ransom pulled the sack upward, revealing Fletcher's face. "Your only mistake, apart from not dyin' when you were told, was bein' stupid enough to leave that saloon alone."

I did *miss him leaving.*

Air snagged in Tate's throat like a fishhook, trying to escape his lips.

He clamped his jaws shut, grinding his molars until his skull ached, and forced the gasp back down into his chest. Wind howled around the ravine, masking the sharp intake of breath that had nearly betrayed him, but his heart hammered against his ribs with the force of a blacksmith's mallet.

Fletcher.

The man kneeling in the snow, his face now bare to the biting wind and the cruelty of Ransom Calder, was the same man who'd slept under Marietta's roof. Whom Nora had stitched up with her own hands. Blood smeared Fletcher's cheek, a dark and wet contrast to the pale skin that hung loose on his skull. One eye had swollen shut, surrounded by flesh the color of a bruised plum.

"C'mon, Fletcher." Ransom leaned down, resting his forearms on his knees. "Make it easy for yourself. Just tell us what you saw."

Fletcher spat a glob of blood into the snow. "Go to hell."

"Wrong answer."

Ransom straightened and nodded to Beau. Without a word, the younger outlaw swung the butt of his rifle. The wood connected with Fletcher's jaw with a sickening *thwack* that carried over the storm to ring in Tate's ears.

Fletcher sprawled onto the frozen ground, his limbs tangling in the loose folds of his coat.

"You think you're some kind of hero?" Ransom kicked Fletcher in the stomach. "You think protectin' a saloon girl and a washed-up rancher makes you a saint?"

Fletcher curled into a ball, wheezing as he struggled to suck in air.

"What did you see? What did you say?"

Tate shifted his weight, digging his boot toes into the ice for leverage. He had the angle; from here, he could put a bullet through Ransom's skull before the man realized death had come for him. Beau would take a second shot. The others—

A hand clamped onto his forearm like an iron band.

Tate whipped his head to the side.

Tamaquah's dark eyes were fixed on the scene below, but his fingers dug through the wool of Tate's sleeve, pinning his arm to the ground.

"Let go!" Tate whispered urgently, frustrated.

"No. Look. *Count.*"

"We take out the leaders," Tate hissed, "and the rest scatter."

"Or kill us before your second bullet leaves the chamber—and the man in the snow dies in the crossfire."

Damn it.

Tamaquah had a point, and Tate hated the cold logic of it: weighing a man's life against the odds of survival. The thought of abandoning Fletcher down there tasted like walking away from the corpses of his parents. Turning his back on Wyatt.

I can't just leave him.

In the clearing, Ransom grabbed Fletcher's lapels and hauled him up. "You got grit, I'll give you that... but grit don't stop a knife."

"Go hang!"

Ransom threw Fletcher back down and looked at Beau. "Get him inside. It's too cold out here for the kind of work we got to do."

THE TEXAS BLIZZARD

Beau grabbed Fletcher by the arms and dragged him through the slush back into the largest tent. Ransom looked at the sky, letting snowflakes melt on his face, before turning to follow.

Tate stared at the canvas flap; he could imagine what came next. The questions would get sharper. The blows would get heavier. They'd use fire, or knives, or just the heavy weight of their fists until Fletcher broke or died.

Tamaquah gestured away from the camp. "We go."

Tate kept his eyes on that flap, willing it to open, wanting Fletcher to somehow burst out and run.

"Tate Hollister." Tamaquah released Tate's arm. "We can do nothing for him here. We are two guns. We need twenty."

"He won't last until we get back."

"Do not underestimate him. He survived a bullet. He survived the snow." Tamaquah pulled on Tate's shoulder. "If we die here, today, no one returns for him. The town has no warning. The fire burns everything."

Tate squeezed his eyes shut. The boy inside him, who wanted to scream and charge, fought against the war-hardened man who knew the value of strategy. The man won, but his victory tasted of ashes. He felt like a coward—a smart one, perhaps, but a coward all the same—choosing his life over the man suffering a few hundred yards away.

Ultimately, it was the thought of the unwitting townsfolk—hunkered down to wait out the storm, unaware of the *real* danger that lurked within the blizzard—that decided him.

Especially since Marietta was among them.

"Alright." Tate pressed his forehead into the snow. "We'll go, but we turn around and come back fast as we can."

They retreated.

Inch by inch, they slithered backward, bellies pressed to the snow, until the lip of the ravine hid the camp from view. Tate moved with the mechanical precision of a soldier, placing his hands and knees where the snow would muffle his weight, but his mind remained in that camp.

Phantom screams drifted on the wind.

When they reached the horses, Tate leaned against the rough bark of a pine and retched. Nothing came up but spit and the sour taste of his own guilt.

Wordlessly, Tamaquah untied the ponies. He didn't offer false comfort or empty words about doing the right thing. He simply handed Tate the reins of his gelding.

Tate swung into the saddle.

Chapter Twenty-One

The rag in Marietta's hand struck the bar with a whip-like *crack*.

She stared across the width of the scarred oak, the heat rising in her chest burning hot enough to melt the frost clinging to the windowpanes.

Tate stood there, dripping grimy snow onto her clean floorboards, looking for all the world like he expected a pat on the back for delivering news that tasted like bile.

They deserted Fletcher.

They'd looked him in the eye and turned their backs as he bled from a wound they'd helped put there.

Images flashed behind her eyes: Fletcher's face, pale and drawn in the guest room upstairs; the way he'd thanked her for the broth, his hand shaking as he held the spoon. Now, that same face lay pressed against the frozen ground, or worse, faced the heat of a branding iron.

"You left him to the coyotes." The words scraped her throat on the way out. "You stood there and watched 'em drag him through the drift like a sack of feed, then turned tail to save your own hide."

Tate thrust a hand through his wet hair, sending droplets flying into the lamplight. "It was two irons against ten, Marietta."

"I don't give a tinker's damn if they had the whole Union army bivouacked in that ravine!" She rounded the corner of the bar. "You don't leave a man behind. Not to *them*."

Cade leaned against the wall near the hearth, wringing his hat in his hands, as Grady stared at his boots.

Cowards, the lot of them.

Tate stepped into her path. He loomed over her, smelling of pine sap, wet wool, and horse sweat. "If we'd drawn down on 'em, we'd be cooling meat—and Fletcher, too—and the town would never know the shot was fired."

"So we trade his blood for time?"

"We trade it for a chance to *win*." He reached for her, but she stepped back before his fingers could graze her sleeve. His hand dropped to his side. "Tamaquah's men ride within the hour. We hit 'em so hard, they won't get back up."

"An hour?" She laughed humorlessly. "You reckon Ransom Calder needs an *hour* to tear a man apart? He'll peel him like an apple soon as you boys saddle your ponies."

She spun on her heel and marched to the gun rack behind the bar. Her fingers curled around the cold steel of the Winchester.

Unlike the promises of men, steel didn't break.

"I'm going." She checked the lever and nodded at the mechanical *click-clack* of a round seating in the chamber. "If you won't fetch him, I will."

"No."

"You don't tell me *no*, Tate Hollister. This is *my* town, *my* saloon, and *my* roof that man slept under."

He grabbed the barrel. "You'll die before you cross the creek."

She tugged, but his grip held.

"Let go," she whispered.

"I can't."

"You sure can."

"The storm out there blinds a man. You can't see ten yards, Marietta. Snow fallin' so thick, you breathe ice. You go out there alone, you won't save Fletcher, just give Calder another hostage!"

"Then I'll go with you."

"No."

"I shoot as straight as any of you!"

"It ain't about that." He wrenched the rifle from her grip and set it back on the bar with a heavy *thud*. "I've seen what they do. I've seen the bodies they leave, and I *won't* see yours among them!"

The wind howled, battering the walls and demanding entry. Inside, the fire popped, spitting sparks against the grate.

He's trying to protect me.

The knowledge sat in her gut, heavy and warm, warring with fury. He saw her as something precious and fragile, something that needed guarding.

He didn't understand; she hadn't been fragile since the day her parents' carriage didn't come home. She hadn't been fragile when she mopped up the blood of the only father figure she'd had left off these floorboards.

"You think I'm scared of dyin'?" She leaned against the bar. "I'm scared of livin' with more regrets, Tate—I got a saloon full of 'em already!"

"Marietta—"

"I see Uncle Everett sitting in that chair in the corner every night. I don't wanna see Fletcher standin' next to him, asking why no one came for him!"

"We *are* going!" Tate placed his hands on the bar, leaning in until his face hovered inches from hers. "Me, Cade, Grady, Tamaquah, and twenty of his best. We surround the ravine and cut off their escape. We end this tonight."

"And if he's already dead?"

"Then we avenge him."

"You need eyes. You need guns. I know that ravine. Uncle Everett took me huntin' there when I was a girl. I know a deer trail that cuts down the back side, comes out right where the dense timber starts. You won't find it in this snow without me."

He covered her hand with his. His palm felt calloused, hard, and warm. She saw the conflict in his eyes, the desire to use every advantage clashing with the terrifying need to keep her safe.

For just a heartbeat, she thought he might yield; then, he pulled her hand away from his coat.

"No."

"Tate—"

"Stay here, and keep that shotgun loaded. Bolt that door, and don't you open it for anyone but us."

"You're makin' a mistake."

"I've made plenty," he retorted, stepping back and pulling the brim of his hat low over his eyes, "but I won't watch you bleed out in the snow. I won't do that again, Marietta—I *can't*."

Oh, but he ain't talkin' about me.

This was about Lynda, she realized. Tate looked at Marietta and saw another ghost in the making, and he'd burn the world down to keep it from forming.

It would be touching—if it weren't so *infuriating*.

"I ain't *her*."

He flinched as if she'd slapped him across the mouth. "I know."

"Then stop treating me like I'm already dead!"

He stared at her—the line of her jaw, the curve of her mouth, the fire she knew burned in her eyes—as if to carve her image into his mind in case the snow swallowed him whole tonight, when she was perfectly capable of being right there with him.

"Alright, boys." He clenched his jaw. "Mount up. We meet Tamaquah at the ridge."

Cade and Grady went to the door, and Tate followed. The wind shrieked as Cade opened the door, a banshee wail that sucked the heat from the room.

Snow swirled in, dancing across the floorboards, as Tate lingered at the threshold. The wind nearly snatched the words from his lips, but Marietta heard them.

"Be careful."

Then, he stepped out, and the heavy oak door slammed shut behind him. The latch caught with a *click*, and quiet descended to fill the saloon once again.

Marietta stood frozen, her hand half-raised, reaching for a man who'd already gone. The fire crackled. The smell of damp wool mingled with stale tobacco smoke in the air, keeping company with the mirages of the men who'd just left.

She paced the length of the bar and looked at Uncle Everett's chair.

He would've let me go.

No, that was a lie. Uncle Everett would've locked her in the cellar before letting her ride against any outlaws, let alone the Bone Orchard Boys. He would've stood in front of the door with his massive arms crossed and told her to hush.

But Uncle Everett is dead, Fletcher is dying, and Tate...

Tate was riding into battle without her.

He'd told her to sit down and wait—and for what? For his horse to come wandering back riderless?

Snatching up her discarded rag, she scrubbed at an obviously clean spot on the bar. Before long, however, she threw the rag down and walked to the window. Tate had told her to be careful, but *careful* only kept you alive; it didn't stop the nightmares or bring justice. Caution didn't stop good men from bleeding out in the dark.

Suddenly, she realized that she'd forgotten to tell him about the sheriff's surprise visit. She'd meant to mention it—and his strange behavior—but anger had driven it from her mind.

Not like it's that important, anyway, just... odd.

Her eyes found the gleaming steel of the Winchester on the bar. Cold. Efficient. The weapon didn't worry about storms, apparitions, or the past; it only cared about the hand that held it and the eye that aimed it.

Not like I got anythin' to lose.

The thought surprised her; she'd thought she had *everything* to lose—but without people to make things matter, nothing had value. The saloon was just wood and glass. Life, if lived in fear, hiding behind a bolted door, wasn't life.

*Except there is something—well, some*one.

She had Tate—the way he looked at her, the memory of his lips on hers, and an ember of hope, fragile as a new shoot in early spring, that something might grow between them once the blood had been washed away—but if he died tonight, she'd lose that too.

If I stay, I might lose him. If I go, I either save him or die with him.

Either of the latter options was better than sitting here, counting ticks of the grandfather clock until the end of the world.

"Lord, forgive me for the folly I'm about to commit."

Having made her decision, she replaced thought with action.

She went to the back room, digging through the chest at the foot of her bed until she found her father's old woolen riding trousers—scratchy, but warm—and pulled them on under her skirt. Then, she found a thick flannel shirt, Uncle Everett's spare coat that smelled of tobacco and comfort, and a heavy scarf.

Back in the main room, she grabbed the Winchester and stuffed a box of cartridges into her coat pocket.

She looked at the map on the wall. The deer trail she'd mentioned to Tate started past an old lightning-struck pine, then twisted through scrub oak, where a horse couldn't go. The gang would be watching the main rim, the approaches a posse would take.

They wouldn't cast a second glance at a goat path buried in snow.

Blowing out the lamps, she plunged the saloon into darkness, save for the dying embers in the hearth.

She looked at Uncle's chair. "I know you'd disapprove, but I ain't waitin' for another carriage that'll never come."

She went to the back door and stepped into the alley by the stables. Wind hit her the moment she glimpsed the sky. Snow swirled into her eyes. Cold bit through the layers of wool.

The tracks of Tate's gelding and the others' mounts were already filling in, becoming shallow dimples in the drifts. In ten minutes, they'd be gone.

Squaring her jaw, she pulled the door shut behind her with a muffled *click*.

Chapter Twenty-Two

The wind had teeth; it chewed through the layers of Tate's wool coat, biting into the scar tissue on his side, and gnawed at the marrow of his bones.

He lowered his head against the gale, squinting until his eyes turned into slits against the onslaught of white.

Ahead, Tamaquah moved like a shadow detached from the earth, slipping between the pines with a silence that mocked Tate's own heavy steps.

Tate placed a boot into the depression Tamaquah had left. Dry, granular snow sifted into the tops of his boots. It melted against his ankles like sugar, trickling down to soak his socks in freezing misery.

Beside him, Cade huddled into his collar, clutching his Winchester as if the rifle could offer warmth. Even Grady, usually impervious to the elements, shivered, his teeth clicking with a rhythmic chatter that sounded too loud in the hush of the storm.

As they crept toward the ravine, woodsmoke cut through the sterile smell of ice. It hooked into Tate's nose, a taunt from the men who sat warm and dry while he and his companions froze.

Voices. Laughter. The *clink* of tin cups. The low rumble of men at ease. The Bone Orchard Boys were close now: just beyond the rise, in that clearing, where the wind couldn't reach them.

Tate crouched behind the trunk of a fallen fir tree. Rough bark scraped his cheek as he peered over the rotting wood.

The bastards sat by their fire, eating fresh venison, while Fletcher lay bleeding somewhere in the dark, injured or dead.

"My blasted fingers don't work." Cade crouched next to him. "Can't feel the doggone trigger."

"Flex 'em. Get the blood movin'."

"If we stay out here much longer, won't need to worry 'bout bullets." Grady made his way to them. "We'll just be statues for 'em to find, come spring."

Tate looked up at the swirling vortex of gray and white above, a heavy lid pressing down on the world. He'd thought the gang would be the only threat tonight, had focused on Ransom Calder and his cruelty, on the man in the bandana and his greed.

He'd forgotten the oldest enemy on the frontier: the cold.

Cold didn't care about justice; it didn't care about revenge, stolen land, or murdered families. It simply took. It slowed the heart, thickened the blood, and dragged a man down into a sleep from which he never woke.

If the temperature dropped another five degrees, they wouldn't even get to the fighting.

We'll die huddled against the trees.

Tate checked his Colt. If they attacked now, would the guns even fire? Or would the hammers fall on dead primers? He imagined storming the camp and pulling the trigger, only to hear a hollow *click* while Ransom Calder laughed and raised his own iron.

Snap

A twig cracked like a whip behind them.

Tate froze; he'd trusted the storm to conceal them, but it could hide the enemy just as easily. A man could walk right up on them in this weather, and they wouldn't know it until the knife slid between their ribs.

Slowly, Tate turned, leveling his Colt at the swirling wall of white behind them. He couldn't see anything but a shifting mosaic created by millions of dancing snowflakes.

Then, a shape detached itself from the gray, resolving into a figure, wrapped in layers of wool, struggling through the drifts.

Tate thumbed the hammer back, aiming for center mass. If this was a scout, Tate had to drop him before he could shout a warning to the camp below.

One shot, hopefully masked by the wind.

The figure stumbled and caught itself on a branch, then looked up—and Tate's breath seized in his lungs, his trigger finger trembling as he lowered the gun.

Green eyes flashed beneath the brim of a snow-caked hat.

Marietta stood ten feet away, clutching her Winchester to her chest. Snow matted the wool of an oversized coat that'd likely belonged to her uncle. Her lips were a pale shade of blue, her cheeks burning with the red of frostnip. She looked small, fragile, and utterly out of place in this frozen hellscape.

Is she insane?

Tate had *told* her to stay put, bolt the door, and *wait*. He'd left her safe in the warmth of the saloon, where the only danger was a drafty window, yet she'd followed him into the teeth of death.

He surged forward. Grabbing her arm, he yanked her behind a pine tree, putting himself between her and the woods. He wanted to shake her, to scream at her until she understood the madness of what she'd done.

"Are you out of your mind?" He brought his face inches from hers. "I told you to stay put!"

She yanked her arm, but he held fast.

"I ain't a dog you can order to *stay*, Tate!"

"You could have died! You could have walked right into a patrol!"

"But I didn't! I'm here!"

"To do what? Freeze? Catch a bullet meant for me?"

If a stray bullet found Marietta out here, if the cold took her, it would be *his* fault. He'd led the charge. He'd opened the door to this violence.

It was Lynda all over again. Lynda, waiting for him on the porch, vulnerable.

"Go back," he growled, "*right now*. Turn around and follow your tracks back to town."

"I ain't goin' nowhere." She shoved at his chest. "I'm here to help."

"You're here to get killed!"

"Quiet!" Tamaquah rushed to them. "The wind changes."

Tate's ears popped as he looked up. The steady drone of the wind dropped an octave, becoming a guttural roar that vibrated the ground. Trees groaned, their branches thrashing overhead.

Then, the whiteout hit.

One second, Tate could make out the ravine, the trees, the shapes of his friends. The next, the world vanished. Snow drove horizontally, millions of ice needles scouring every inch of exposed skin and filling Tate's nose, mouth, and eyes. The air froze solid, unbreathable.

"Cade! Grady!"

No answer.

Thankfully, he was still holding Marietta, so he hauled her against him, wrapping his arm around her waist. She stumbled, her boots slipping on the ice hidden beneath the fresh powder. She felt tiny against the magnitude of the storm.

A muffled *boom* sounded in the distance.

He clenched harder. "Don't let go!"

"I can't see!"

Truthfully, neither could he; up was down, left was right. The ravine lay somewhere to his right, and enemy fire waited on the left.

Or was it the other way around?

He spun, searching for Tamaquah—anyone.

Nothing but white: endless, suffocating white.

We won't survive without shelter...

He pictured the map, dredging Fletcher's description into a mind gone sluggish with cold. He'd mentioned an outbuilding—a storage shed, set apart from the main camp, up near the tree line. It had to be close.

He dragged Marietta forward. "Move!"

They stumbled. He kept one arm around her, the other held out in front of him, fingers splayed, searching for anything solid. The wind tried to tear them apart. It shoved and battered them, trying to knock them off their feet.

Tate's boot caught on a root, and he went down, dragging Marietta with him. They hit the snow hard. The cold burned his face. He scrambled up, hauling her with him.

"Keep moving!"

If we stop, we die.

He pushed forward, head down, plowing through thigh-high drifts. Every step required monumental effort. His legs burned as his lungs screamed for air that wasn't filled with ice.

His hand struck rough-hewn timber—a wall.

Thank God.

Splinters dug through his gloves as he felt along the planks, searching for a corner, a door, anything. Marietta huddled against his back. Finally, he found a latch, but the iron had frozen shut. He hammered it desperately with the butt of his Colt. Once. Twice.

The ice shattered.

He kicked the door open, then shoved Marietta inside. Following, he threw his weight against the door, forcing it shut even as the wind fought to keep it open. With a final strained grunt, he slammed it home and dropped the wooden crossbar into place.

Silence—comparatively, at least.

The gale still howled outside, battering the structure, but the piercing, howling whistle of the wind was gone. Inside, the still, heavy air smelled of old hay, harness oil, and dust.

Tate sagged against the door, gasping for breath, then slid down the wood until he hit the dirt floor. "Marietta?"

"I'm... I'm here."

Tate nodded and strained to hear beyond the rage of the weather outside, hoping for voices, footsteps, anything. He couldn't remember how far this shed was from camp; the outlaws could very well be right outside the door.

Fifty yards? A hundred?

Worse, the outlaws might actually use the shed for something. If someone came to fetch anything, Tate and Marietta might as well be cornered rats.

Her coat rustled as she moved closer. "Tate." Her hand found his arm. Violent tremors wracked her entire frame. "I'm freezing."

He guided her to a pile of ancient hay in a corner. It smelled musty, but offered insulation from the frozen ground. He sat down, pulling her into the space between his legs, wrapping his heavy coat around both of them. It wasn't exactly appropriate, but no one was here to see. Even if they had been, he'd tell them where to go with their opinions.

This is about survival.

Burrowing into him, Marietta rested her head against his chest.

"You fool," he murmured into her hair. "You damn fool."

"Don't start."

"You shouldn't be here."

"Neither should you."

He rubbed her arms, trying to push the warmth of his own blood into hers.

This is a nightmare.

He'd tried so hard to keep the violence of his world away from her saloon. He'd built walls, pushed her away, lied to himself about his feelings, all to prevent this exact scenario.

And yet, he'd failed; she was here, trapped in a shed surrounded by killers, with a blizzard burying them alive.

He rested his chin on the top of her head. "If they find us…"

"I know."

She shifted, pressing her ear against his heart. He wondered if she could hear the terror beating there. He didn't fear for himself—he'd made his peace with death long ago—but for her.

"Tate?"

"Yeah?"

"I ain't sorry I came."

He closed his eyes. He felt the urge to scold her again, but the fight drained out of him quickly, leaving only cold and fear.

"I figured."

He squeezed her tighter as the storm raged on, sealing them in what could very well become their tomb; at that moment, for the first time in fourteen years, Tate Hollister prayed. Not for vengeance. Not for justice.

He prayed for morning. For the snow to hide them. That the shaking of the woman in his arms wouldn't be the last thing he ever felt.

He listened to the wood groan. They were alone.

And the devils waited just outside the door.

Chapter Twenty-Three

Thickening ice coated the brim of Amos Sharpe's hat, layer by layer, until the felt bowed, pressing against his brow like a crown of lead.

He tightened his grip on the reins.

His gloved fingers had long since lost any sensation of the leather, reduced to stiff claws that obeyed his commands only through rote memory. Beneath him, his bay gelding threw its head against the biting gale, snorting out clouds of steam that vanished instantly into the white void.

Amos drove his spurs into the gelding's flanks.

The town of Sherman sat miles behind him now, a huddle of timber and fear lost in the whiteout. He pictured the citizens, huddled in the Golden Fleece or gathered around their hearths. They'd be staring into the flames, chafing their hands, murmuring about their sheriff.

In their minds, Amos cut a figure of marble and iron, jaw set against the elements, eyes piercing the storm to find the lost sheep.

He exhaled.

Let them construct their effigies. It kept their heads down, the tax levies paid on time, and the hats tipped when he strode down the boardwalk.

The trail—if this erasure of geography could even be called a trail—led north. Here, the land became traitorous. Rolling plains buckled into rugged country, where ravines cut deep scars into the earth, hidden by the treacherous blanket of snow.

Amos knew the land: where drop-offs lurked, where the wind had tunneled through rock faces. He knew it better than the trappers who drank away their profits in the spring, the ranchers who claimed ownership with ink on paper, and maybe even the Comanche.

If only Hollister wasn't so damned stubborn.

Why did some men insist on digging until the shovel broke? Tate Hollister had been stripped of his cattle, his home, and his standing. Anyone with a functional instinct for survival would've read the writing on the wall, packed his saddlebags, sold the charred timber of his homestead for scrap, and ridden toward the Pacific.

But no. No, he has to make a stand.

And currently, because of that refusal to bend, Amos was losing the feeling in his toes as he rode through a white hell, all to verify a corpse.

The gelding stumbled again, sliding outward on a patch of hidden slick-rock. Amos checked the animal with a violent jerk of the reins, keeping his seat with the unconscious balance of a man who'd spent more of his life on leather than on wood or dirt.

Then, he patted the horse's neck. "Step sure."

I need to see the body.

Reports were sloppy things. Rumors drifted into town like dead leaves—whispers of a posse forming in the high country, talk of Comanche riders moving in the storm, tales of a man surviving a bullet to the gut.

Amos pulled back on the reins, bringing the horse to a halt.

Tracks marred the snow.

The depressions were faint, blurred by the relentless fall, but the edges remained jagged. A group had passed here, moving heavy and fast. Unshod ponies. The corners of his mouth twitched upward beneath the scarf.

So, the whispers have some merit to them.

Tamaquah—the Comanche he'd sent Ransom to bargain with, for all the good it had done—had come down from the high country. His people were starving, their buffalo ranges fenced off or slaughtered, their hunting parties harassed until they snapped. A dog backed into a corner didn't negotiate; it bit the first hand that reached for it.

Amos's father used to say that you couldn't build a house on a swamp. Of course, he'd been a weak man, a man who wept over poetry and died with a liver full of cheap whiskey and a heart full of regrets.

The old man had been wrong: you *could* build on a swamp—you just had to drain it first.

The Bone Orchard Boys raided the ranchers. The ranchers blamed the Comanche or the government. The Comanche blamed the settlers. They fought each other, bleeding into the dirt, and in the confusion, land values plummeted. Once panic set in, the man with cash and a plan could step in to collect the shattered pieces for pennies on the dollar.

Amos spurred the horse on, following the faint, jagged trail toward the ridge.

He'd warned Marietta. He truly had. She ran a clean establishment and watered her whiskey less than the others, but she'd just looked at him with green eyes and refused to blink. It was the look of someone who'd burn the house down with herself inside rather than hand over the key.

The wind roared louder as the terrain rose, pitching upward toward the jagged spine of the country. He was nearing the ridge that overlooked a deep ravine where trappers used to camp in winters past.

He moved his right hand to his hip, brushing snow from the leather holster where his heavy Dragoon pistol waited for him. Ideally, the gun would stay cold.

Just as he reached the crest of the ridge, his horse stumbled sideways.

Amos dismounted, grabbed the reins near the bit, forcing the animal's head down, and tied it to the trunk of a wind-twisted pine that clung to the rock like a desperate hand.

Keeping low, Amos moved to the edge of the drop-off and toward the cluster of trees in the distance.

A cauldron of swirling milk awaited him. The world ended five feet in front of him. But sound... sound traveled strangely in the cold.

Crack.

A gunshot. Muffled, flattened by the heavy air, but unmistakable.

Then another. A rapid exchange. The *thud-thud-thud* of heavy caliber fire answering the sharper *snap* of rifles.

Amos crouched by a boulder, squinting, until the moisture on his eyelashes froze into tiny needles.

In the belly of the storm, the rats were eating each other. Tate and his little band against Ransom and his wolves. The Comanche were likely there too, shadows moving in the blindness, loosing arrows at anything that moved.

He could visualize the mechanics of it. The confusion. The utter lack of tactical cohesion. Men shooting at muzzle flashes, killing each other over a patch of frozen dirt that wouldn't matter in a hundred years.

He made a sound in his throat—a dry, rasping noise that might have been a laugh if there had been any humor in it.

Let them bleed.

Let Hollister spend his ammunition. Let Ransom thin the herd of Indians. Every man who died down there was one less variable for Sheriff Amos Sharpe to calculate in the spring. If Tate died, the ranchers lost their spine. If Tamaquah died, the Comanche dissolved into factional infighting. If Ransom lost a few men... well, hired guns were a renewable resource in Texas.

Fate's doing the labor. I just gotta write the report.

He could see the headline now: *Tragedy in the Mountains!* The story beneath would tell of a brave posse getting lost in the storm, only to die in a savage ambush—and cast *him* as the tragic hero of the tale. *The sheriff arrived too late to save them, but in time to secure the peace.*

It had the right cadence to it. The town would mourn. They'd look to him for reassurance. He'd stand on the steps of the jailhouse and give a speech about resilience and the need for stricter adherence to the law, slowly tightening his grip all the while.

He turned to head back to his horse.

Sure, he hadn't *seen* anything, but he'd heard, and that would be enough. The outcome didn't matter as much as the event itself.

Then, movement caught his eye.

Two shapes were struggling through deep drifts near the tree line. They didn't move with the stealth of warriors or the confidence of men in control; they lurched and collided with one another.

Reaching into his pocket, he withdrew a brass spyglass and extended the tube with a *snap*. He raised it, pressing the eyepiece against his orbital bone, and focused on the gray blurs.

The lenses cleared, revealing a man and a woman.

Amos recognized the man's coat—heavy, military cut, stained dark on the shoulder. Tate Hollister. He was dragging the woman, his arm around her waist, half-carrying her through the snow. And the woman... even bundled in layers of wool, he knew the set of those shoulders.

Amos lowered the glass slowly.

So, she came.

Despite the logic. Despite the blizzard. Marietta had ridden out to throw herself onto the pyre with her broken rancher.

He raised the glass again. They were heading for the old storage shed near the rim, a rotting structure barely fit for kindling.

Amos's hand moved to his hip. His fingers curled around the walnut grip of the Dragoon. He drew the weapon.

He could end it. He could put a bullet in Hollister's spine and watch him drop face-first into the drift. Then, he shifted his aim to Marietta. He could kill her first, just to mess with Hollister for being such a stubborn son of a gun. Watch him cry for a bit before putting him out of his misery.

Amos's finger tightened on the trigger.

His stomach tightened. A sour fluid rose in his throat. She had *value*. A mind for numbers. She could've run that saloon for ten more years, paying him his percentage, keeping the men sedated with whiskey and cards.

A good asset.

Yet, here she was, throwing herself into the grinder for a man with nothing to offer but a grave.

Why do people insist on destroying themselves? Why choose the hard road when you can just pay the toll to walk the paved one?

He watched them reach the shed. Hollister hammered the rusted latch with a fist that looked like a block of ice. Then, they shoved the door open and tumbled inside, vanishing into the darkness, sealing themselves in the wooden box.

Amos held his aim on the door for a long moment; then, exhaling slowly, he lowered the hammer of the pistol with his thumb.

The wind pushed at his back insistently, urging him to return to the warmth of his office and the bottle of brandy in his desk drawer. But he lingered, staring at the wooden shack almost buried in the snow.

He *could* kill Hollister. It would be easy. An execution.

Then, he could drag Marietta back to town. Spin a story—he found her wandering, delirious, the sole survivor of a massacre. She'd be in his debt, broken by the loss, pliable, ready to be molded.

He ran the scenario through his mind, checking for flaws.

No.

She'd seen too much. If she survived, she would talk. Scream. Ask questions. Judge him with those green eyes and see the cracks in the mask he'd spent a lifetime perfecting.

He shook his head.

Not my fault she put her bet on Hollister.

Besides, that shed would *not* survive this storm. The roof sagged under a foot of snow. Gaps in the thin walls where wind had stripped the wood were visible, even from this distance. No fire. No food. The temperature was dropping by the minute. The sun was failing, and the true cold—the killing cold—was coming.

The storm would do what a bullet would, only slower.

Let the cold work.

Let the frost creep into the cracks in the walls. Let them huddle together in the dark as the numbness started in their fingers and worked its way to their hearts. Let them watch each other turn blue.

A poetic end for a romance built on vengeance.

He collapsed the spyglass with a sharp *snap* and shoved it back into his pocket.

"Goodbye, Marietta."

Turning his back on the cabin, the fighting, and the two souls shivering in the dark, he walked back to his horse. The gelding tossed its head as he approached, stamping a hoof into the snow.

"Easy." Amos checked the cinch and tightened it one notch. "We're going."

He mounted and rode off.

Chapter Twenty-Four

Wind shrieked against the rough-hewn planks of the shed, demanding entry with the fury of a thousand screaming devils.

Marietta huddled in the corner, pulling her knees to her chest; the damp hay beneath her offered little protection from the frozen earth, and shivers raked her spine. Her teeth clicked together in a rhythm she couldn't control, a staccato beat that echoed the rattling of the door latch Tate had barred.

She stared at her hands. In the gloom, they looked like claws. They trembled violently. She tried to clench them, to force blood back into the stiff knuckles, but her muscles rebelled. The cold had settled deep beneath her skin, burrowing into the marrow of her bones like a parasite.

Crack.

The memory of the gunshot they'd heard replayed in her mind. It hadn't sounded like the sharp snap of a Winchester or the roar of a Colt. It sounded flat. Final. A punctuation mark on a sentence she hadn't wanted to read.

Who got hit?

Cade? Grady? Tamaquah? Or had the bullet found Fletcher, finishing the job the Bone Orchard Boys had started yesterday?

Tate paced the small enclosure like a caged tiger. Three steps to the wall, turn, three steps back. Even in the shadows, tension radiated from him in waves, heat that offered no warmth.

He paused at the door, pressing his ear against the wood.

She trembled. "You catch wind of anythin'?"

He shook his head without turning. "Nothin'."

"Maybe... maybe the snow muffled it. Reckon they cut loose?"

He pushed off the door and resumed his pacing. "Or maybe they're buzzard meat. Maybe we're the only ones left."

She didn't want to consider that possibility. If she let it take root, the walls of this shed would close in until they crushed her. She focused on the rusted lantern hook on the ceiling, on the smell of old harness oil and moldering straw. Anything to keep the image of Uncle Everett's empty chair from merging with the image of Tate's friends lying in the snow.

Tate loomed over her, a dark silhouette against the gray light filtering through the cracks in the wood.

"You shouldn't be here."

"We done chewed this bone already."

"I told you." He clenched his fists at his sides. "I told you to bolt the door. To wait. But you had to come. You had to play the hero."

"I ain't playin' nothin'." She pushed herself up. "I rode out 'cause I wasn't fixin' to sit there countin' seconds 'til you *didn't* come back."

"And look where it got you!" He swept an arm around the dilapidated shed. "Trapped. Freezin'. Surrounded by men who'd put you in the ground for a dollar. Is this better, Marietta? Is this what you had a hankerin' for?"

"I wanted to help!"

"You're a millstone 'round my neck!"

Tears pricked her eyes, but she blinked them back. She wouldn't cry. She wouldn't let him see her break.

"I know the trail," she whispered. "I got this far."

"And now, you're boxed in." He stepped closer, invading her space, his breath pluming in the cold air between them. "If they ferret us out… if they drag us out of here…"

"Tate—"

"I ain't got the stomach for it. I can't watch them hurt you."

She looked down.

He reached out, gripping her shoulders. His fingers dug into the wool of Uncle Everett's coat. "I lost Lynda. I put my kin in the ground. If I lose you—if I have to stand there and watch the light go out of your eyes 'cause I couldn't keep you off the trail…"

He choked.

Marietta looked up at him. "You ain't losin' me."

"You don't know that."

"I know I'm standin' right here." She lifted a hand and put it on his chest. "I couldn't stay behind, Tate. If I'd've let you ride out alone, knowin' I might never lay eyes on you again… that would've killed me just as sure as lead."

He covered her hand with his own.

"I wanted to keep you safe."

"I don't *want* 'safe.' I want to be with *you*."

She hadn't meant to say it, not like that, but the cold stripped away pretenses. They stood on the edge of a knife, balanced between life and death, and there was no room for lies.

Tate let out a shuddering breath. He leaned his forehead against hers. The brim of his hat bumped hers, knocking it back. His skin felt ice-cold, but his breath warmed her face.

"You stubborn woman."

"Mule-headed man."

For a long moment, they simply breathed together, two daylight creatures huddled against the encroaching dark. Then, he lifted his head slightly. His gaze searched hers, traveling from her eyes to her lips and back again.

"We need to stay warm," he murmured, pulling back just enough to break the spell.

"Yeah." She wrapped her arms around herself. "We do."

They returned to the corner with the hay.

Tate sat down, his back against the wall, and pulled her down with him. He opened his heavy coat, wrapping one side around her, cocooning them together. She settled between his legs, leaning her back against his chest.

It wasn't proper.

The matrons of Sherman would've fainted dead away to see Marietta Walker tangled up with a man she wasn't married to. But those women were sitting in warm houses with roaring fires. Here, preserving propriety would mean death.

She rested her head on his shoulder. His arm came around her waist, holding her tight.

Heat seeped from him into her. It started as a faint trickle, then grew, thawing the ice in her veins. She closed her eyes.

The smell of him—tobacco, leather, the faint metallic tang of gun oil—filled her senses, pushing back the musty odor of the shed.

Hours dragged by, but the storm refused to break. It pounded the roof, finding loose shingles to rattle. Drafts snaked through cracks in the walls, ghostly fingers searching for warmth to steal.

Marietta dozed. Dreams fragmented and scattered.

Uncle Everett pouring whiskey. A rope tightening around a neck. Snow falling in a black room.

She jerked awake to find that the cold had deepened. Her toes felt like stones in her boots. The arm that should've been around her waist was missing.

Tate stood by the narrow window slit on the far wall. He'd scraped the frost from a single pane of glass to peer out into the white void. His body held the tension of a drawn bowstring.

"Tate?"

He raised a hand.

She scrambled to her feet. Moving to his side, she peered past his shoulder. The world outside existed only in shades of gray. The snow fell in sheets, a relentless curtain that obscured the trees, the ravine, the sky.

"What is it?" she whispered.

"I saw light—a lantern." He pointed toward the tree line, where the forest swallowed the clearing. "Moving. Low to the ground."

She squinted. "Are you sure? Maybe it was the wind moving a branch."

"I know what I saw."

"Could it be one of our friends?"

"Maybe." He didn't sound convinced. "Or maybe it's the sheriff."

Marietta frowned. "Sharpe?"

"Tamaquah left a scout near town." Tate turned from the window. "He saw Sharpe ride out before the storm hit."

"I meant to tell you before, but... Well, Sharpe came to the saloon, which is strange enough, but he was acting odd, too."

"How so?"

"He seemed... capable—not like the man who sits behind a desk and polishes his star." She breathed quietly. "He handled some drunks at the saloon like they were naughty children."

Tate looked back at the window. "Odd timin' to ride out, right after us. In this weather, only a fool lookin' to buy the farm would be leavin' town—or, more likely, a mongrel hell-bent on killin' sheep."

She blinked. "You think he's with them?"

"A lazy man don't suddenly find ambition when the snow starts fallin'." Tate moved away from the window. "I think he knew exactly where we were goin'."

Marietta shivered. She remembered Sharpe's eyes in the saloon. Watchful. Calculating. He hadn't looked like a concerned lawman; he'd looked like a man assessing a threat.

"If he's out there," she said, "and he has a lantern..."

"He's not alone." Tate checked his Colt, spinning the cylinder. "That, or he doesn't care who might see him."

They waited. Every creak of wood sounded like a boot step, every gust of wind like a voice. Tate stood guard by the door, gun in hand, while Marietta crouched in the hay, gripping her Winchester until her fingers cramped.

Eventually, when the lantern didn't return, her adrenaline faded, leaving crushing exhaustion in its wake.

Tate slid down the wall to sit by the door, then patted the space beside him. "Come here. You need sleep."

"I can't."

"If they come, you need to be clear-headed enough to act—which means your noggin needs rest."

She crawled to him. They resumed their huddle, like terrified children hiding from the monster under the bed.

But the monster wasn't under the bed—he rode a horse and wore a badge, and he waited in the snow.

***

Sleep claimed her in fits and starts, and she woke to silence.

The roaring had stopped. The wind no longer battered the walls. Pale light seeped through cracks in the planks, illuminating dust motes hanging in the still air.

Tate was already awake. He stood by the door, peering through a knot in the wood. His face looked haggard, stubble darkening his jaw, his eyes rimmed with red.

"Storm broke," he rasped.

Marietta pushed herself up. "Is it clear?"

"Seems to be."

He lifted the wooden bar and pushed the door.

Bright, blinding white assaulted her eyes, and she shielded her face, blinking against the glare.

The world had transformed. The ugliness of the night, the terror and darkness, lay buried under a pristine blanket of white. Pines drooped under the weight of it beneath a cloudless blue sky. It looked peaceful. Innocent.

Then, she looked down.

Ten yards from the shed, a mound of snow broke the smooth perfection of the glittering carpet. A patch of dark color, stark against the white, caught her eye. A hand. Brown skin, frozen rigid, reaching toward the sky.

"Tate."

He followed her gaze. Cursing, he waded through the snow, and Marietta followed. Tate brushed the snow away from the mound.

A man lay, face down, wearing buckskins and a fur-lined coat. A quiver spilled arrows across his back.

Marietta covered her mouth.

One of Tamaquah's scouts.

Tate rolled the body over. The man's eyes stared open, glazed with frost, fixed on a point in the distance. There was no blood on his front. No sign of a struggle.

Tate turned the man's head.

"Here." He pointed to the base of the skull.

A small, neat hole marred the skin. The powder burns around the wound stood out black against the copper flesh.

"Executed," Tate said. "Shot from behind. Close range."

Bile rose in Marietta's throat, but she swallowed it down. "The gunshot we heard."

"Yeah."

"But... only one body?"

"One we've found." Tate stood up, scanning the tree line. "The others might have scattered, or they might be under the drifts."

He looked back at the dead scout.

"This wasn't a fight, Marietta. This was *murder*. A man doesn't let an enemy get this close behind him unless he doesn't *know* he's an enemy."

The realization hit her like a bucket of icy water.

"The sheriff," she whispered.

"He rides up, wearing a badge, and says he's looking for the posse." Tate shook his head. "The scout lowers his bow and turns to point the way, and... *Bang*."

She looked at the tracks leading away from the body. The tail end of the storm had partially softened them, but they led toward the ravine—the direction in which Tate had seen a lantern in the night.

"He's hunting us."

Tate grabbed her arm. "We have to go."

"Where?"

"Away from here. If Sharpe met up with Calder... If they know we're alive..."

Marietta looked toward the tree line, where pines cast long, blue shadows across the snow.

What—?

"Tate." She pointed.

A flash of yellow, faint in the morning sun, flickered deep within the woods, then vanished: a lantern, quickly extinguished—or light reflected off polished metal?

A star, perhaps...?

Tate grabbed her hand, pulling her toward the ravine, away from the trees, away from the shed.

"Run!"

Chapter Twenty-Five

Wind scoured the ravine, scrubbing away their tracks and filling the hollows with fresh powder. Tate pushed through the drifts, ducking his head against the gale. Behind him, the *squeak* of boots on fresh, deep snow told him Marietta was matching him step for step, though he knew the cold must be gnawing on her bones just as it chewed on his.

As they moved away from the shed and the dead scout, Tate cursed, hating the blinding whiteout and deafening silence. Most of all, though, he despised the sour feeling in his gut, like he'd eaten spoiled meat.

The image of that execution-style hole in the base of the man's skull shone in Tate's mind brighter than any lantern. Sharpe had done that—the man who polished a star while the town bled had ridden out, found a warrior with his guard down, and put a bullet in him.

What kind of man does it take to kill a stranger in cold bloodlike that?

Tate scanned the trees. Pines stood like sentinels wrapped in shrouds, offering enough cover for a hundred riflemen. He swept his gaze left, then right. Nothing moved but the wind and the falling ice.

They needed to find Cade.

Tamaquah wouldn't know about Sharpe; if *he* found his scout and saw that wound, he'd likely assume that Tate's group had betrayed him. If Cade and Grady stood in the middle of that misunderstanding, they wouldn't last five minutes.

You dealt from the bottom of the deck with that one, Sharpe.

Tate pushed the thought down. Regret served no purpose now, neither warming the blood nor loading a rifle. He forced his legs through the knee-deep powder toward the ridge. It'd been nearly a full day since the group had separated; chances were, the storm had pushed Cade, Grady, or the Comanche down into that ravine. Tate needed a vantage point to check.

They crested the rise, and Tate squinted as the wind hit them full force, screaming over the lip of the canyon.

Below, the ground flattened out, and the pristine snow had been churned, trampled, and kicked into a slurry of mud and ice.

Marietta grabbed his elbow and indicated a cluster of boulders down the slope. "There."

Tate nodded and made his way down slowly, digging his heels in to control his descent. The bottom of the ravine looked as though a stampede had passed through. Hoofprints gouged the earth. Boots had slipped and skidded.

He knelt by a patch of dark, sickly pink snow. Blood—not a spray, but a smear, as if some heavy, wounded beast had been dragged through the ravine. The marks disappeared into the trees, mingling with the tracks of unshod ponies and iron-shod horses.

He touched the stain. *Frozen solid.*

Spent brass glittered in the weak sunlight. He picked up a .44-40 rifle cartridge, the metal agonizingly cold against his fingertips.

Cade had fired this; Tate knew how Cade kept his Henry rifle clean, how the ejector threw the brass high and to the right.

Moving quickly now, Tate found another casing, then another—and, ultimately, a pile of them, clustered behind the cover of the boulders.

Cade had made a stand here.

So where is he now?

Tate spun in a circle, rifle raised, searching the tree line, the ruins, the sky. No bodies. No horses. Just blood and brass.

"Outlaws took 'em." Marietta stood over a set of drag marks that led away from boulders. "Or they lit a shuck."

"Cade wouldn't run." Tate pocketed the first casing. "Not if he was throwin' lead. That boy plants himself like an oak."

Then, he spotted something snagged on a low bush. A strip of fabric. Red wool.

Tamaquah wore a shirt of that color beneath his furs.

Tate plucked the fabric from the thorns. It hadn't torn by accident; it had been cut clean, sliced away with a blade.

"They tangled here." Tate looked it over. "Tamaquah's men and the gang. Maybe Sharpe, too."

"You reckon they're…"

Marietta trailed off, but he had a good idea what she'd almost asked.

Reckon they're dead?

If Cade or Grady lay under a drift somewhere, cold and stiff, Tate would burn this entire mountain range to the ground. He'd find every man responsible and send them to hell before the sun set.

"No." He shoved the fabric into his pocket. "No bodies means they took 'em upright."

He examined the tracks again. They headed north, toward the box canyon where an abandoned supply barn stood. While old, the sturdy oak-and-stone structure had been designed to hold feed through the winter; if a man needed to hole up, it was an ideal place to take shelter.

He gestured in that direction. "Let's go."

They moved into the timber. Trees grew thickly here, blocking out the worst of the wind, even with the tunnel effect, but every snap of a twig sounded like a gunshot. Every shifting branch looked like a man raising a weapon.

Tate placed his feet carefully. Kept his breathing shallow. Watched for spooked birds, squirrels, or anything that might signal an intruder.

But the woods remained quiet. *Too* quiet.

Marietta followed close. She didn't complain or ask to rest. She held her Winchester across her chest, scanning the flank, watching his back.

She had grit—he gave her that—more grit, in fact, than half the men he'd served with.

And he'd dragged her square into the kill box.

Stop it. Survive now, regret later.

They tracked the group for an hour. The signs grew fresher: broken bushes and branches; fresh horse droppings that steamed faintly in the frigid air; a discarded bandage, stained yellow and red.

The terrain dipped, and the trees opened up into the narrow valley that fed into the box canyon.

Tate stopped and held up a hand.

Smoke drifted through the treetops, smelling of pine pitch and tobacco.

He signaled Marietta to get low. They crouched in the underbrush. Snow soaked into their knees. Tate crept forward behind a fallen log until a massive structure came into view, gray with age, its roof sagging under several feet of snow: the supply barn. It sat in the center of a clearing, backed against the sheer rock wall of the canyon.

A dozen or so horses stood tethered to a hitching rail out front, heads low, steam rising from their flanks—as though recovering from a hard ride—their saddles still on, rifles in scabbards.

No sentries on the perimeter.

Now, that just ain't right.

Sharpe wasn't a fool. He wouldn't leave his back door open unless he was expecting company, and Tate had already walked into *that* particular trap once.

"Tate," Marietta breathed into his ear, "I don't see any Comanche ponies."

"Yeah. Cade and Grady's horses aren't here, either."

"Reckon they slipped the noose?"

"I wouldn't bet a bent nickel on anything right now." He shook his head. "Stay here. I need to see—"

"No." She clenched his forearm. "If you go, *I* go."

He looked at her hand; her knuckles had gone white against the wool of his sleeve. She was his anchor. His liability. His reason for breathing. The thought of taking her from the relative safety of the trees turned his blood to slush.

"I need a rifle on my flank, not a shadow on my hoof. If they bust out, guns blazin', I need you to pour it on 'em."

She looked at the barn, then back at him. "I—"

He pressed his forehead to hers. *"Trust me."*

He poured every ounce of his soul into those two words. He *needed* her to trust him, even though he didn't trust himself. She had to believe he had a plan, even though he was making it up as he went along.

Just to keep her safe.

"Fine," she hissed, "but if you get yourself killed—"

"I won't."

He had no way of knowing that, of course—he didn't know anything except that he had to cross that clearing—but that didn't matter.

He moved, keeping low, sprinting from tree to stump until he reached the side of the barn. Then, he pressed his back against the rough wood and listened.

Voices. Muffled. Indistinct. A low rumble of conversation.

No screaming. No sounds of torture. Just talk.

He crept toward a gap in the wall, where a plank had rotted away near the foundation. Then, he knelt in the slush and put his eye to the hole.

A lantern hung from a beam, casting a circle of yellow light in the center of the vast, dusty space. Hay bales lay scattered, and shadows moved in the gloom.

Ransom Calder sat on a crate, cleaning his fingernails with a knife. Beside him, Beau leaned against a post, smoking a cigarette. Other men, whose names Tate didn't know, lingered about. No trace of Cade, Grady, or any of the Comanche.

Then, movement near the lantern caught his eye.

Another man stepped into the light, walking with a heavy stride. He wore a long duster coat with snow melting on the shoulders. Taking off his hat, he slapped it against his leg, sending a spray of water into the dust.

A silver star gleamed on his shoulder, polished to a mirror shine.

I'm seein' it with my own eyes, and I still can't believe it's Sharpe, of all people.

However, it wasn't just the betrayal that enraged Tate; it was the *arrogance* of it. Sharpe wore the star like a costume, a shield for his rot, while he walked with the confidence of a king in his castle.

Tate wanted to smash that lantern and burn the barn down with all of them inside.

Walking over to Calder, Sharpe reached into his pocket, pulled out a silver flask, and offered it to the outlaw. Calder grinned as he accepted it and took a long pull. They *laughed.* The lawman shared whiskey with outlaws while Tate's friends were scattered in the snow.

The sound of that laughter stripped the last layer of civility from Tate's soul. If the law meant nothing, then *justice* meant nothing. Tate had a gun in his hand; if he shot fast enough, he could get them both before the other outlaws rushed him.

Sitting in his office, Sharpe had listened to Tate plead for help and watched Marietta cry for her uncle—all while counting the money he'd made on their blood. He'd killed Tamaquah's scout in cold blood, just to sow discord between Tate and the Comanche. He'd orchestrated the ambush.

No, stop focusin' on the betrayal.

He took a deep breath.

They ain't got no prisoners. I gotta go back to Marietta and go look for—

Sharpe turned to look straight at the gap where Tate crouched.

Tate blinked.

That... That ain't possible. I haven't made a peep!

Sharpe couldn't possibly have *seen* him through a tiny hole, especially with the damned lantern glaring inside.

"Come on out, Tate—there's one spyin' hole, and I see the gleam of your eye in it," Sharpe smirked. "And I saw you take Marietta into that shed with you, so go on and bring her, too. Coffee's hot."

Tate froze as the barn door creaked open.

Calder stepped out, pistol drawn, flanked by two men with rifles. They aimed at the trees, though—thankfully—they didn't seem to know *exactly* where Marietta hid.

Rifle in hand, Tate stood and crept slowly away from the barn.

Then, Sharpe himself stepped out and smiled at Tate *again*. "No need to run off, Tate. Call the girl in. We're all just breakin' bread here."

Chapter Twenty-Six

Bark rough as a rasp dug into Marietta's cheek as she pressed herself against the pine. Cold seeped through the layers of wool she wore, an insidious chill that stiffened her fingers around the receiver of the Winchester.

The ice in her veins, however, came not from the weather but the sight before her: Tate backing away as Sharpe smiled at him.

Sharpe didn't look like a monster. That was the worst of it. He didn't have horns or a tail. His duster flapped gently in the wind, and his smile belonged to a favorite uncle greeting kin at a Sunday supper.

"Stow the theatrics, Tate." Sharpe showed his open palms, the picture of reasonable authority, while Ransom Calder stood behind him like a wolf on a leash. "Uncock that iron. We're all drinkin' from the same trough here."

What a load of...

The man who'd polished his star while her uncle bled out on the floorboards now stood shoulder to shoulder with the butcher who'd ordered it—no, wrong. *Sharpe* had ordered it.

She tightened her grip on the rifle stock.

If she moved, they'd see her. If she stayed, though, she'd leave Tate exposed.

"Same trough?" Tate scoffed. "I see you breakin' bread with the man who torched my homestead. I see you standin' beside the cur who put a slug in Fletcher Avery. Tell me, Sheriff—does Judas pay in silver or lead these days?"

Chuckling, Sharpe stepped off the threshold and into the snow. "You stare at the manure, Tate, and miss the horse entirely."

"What the hell are you babblin' about?"

"I keep the peace. That's the *job*." Sharpe hooked his thumbs into his gun belt. "Sometimes, survival means swallowin' a little bile and shakin' hands with men you wouldn't invite to Sunday supper, just to ensure the town don't freeze or starve."

Lies.

Oiled lies slithered from his mouth. He spoke of peace while running a slaughterhouse.

Marietta watched Calder smirk, a twist of lips that promised violence, and knew the sheriff didn't believe a word of his own sermon. He didn't care about peace, only control, the coin in his pocket, and the power in his fist.

"That what you call gut-shootin' a Comanche scout in the snow?" Tate moved further backward. "Sellin' out your neighbors to a pack of saddle-tramps is *survival*? You ain't keepin' order, Sharpe. You're sellin' us by the pound."

The sheriff's smile frayed at the edges. It didn't vanish all at once, but the mask slipped. The paternal warmth drained from his eyes, leaving the flat stare of a shark scenting blood in the water. He sighed, a long exhalation of white steam, as if Tate were an unruly child refusing to learn a simple lesson.

"I *tried*, Hollister." Sharpe pinched the bridge of his nose. "I gave you *every* chance to walk away. I warned Marietta, too—told you both to leave it be—but you... You just had to play the hero in a story that don't *have* one."

"I ain't no hero," Tate growled, "just the man who's gonna put you in the ground."

"You're a spent casing. Nothin' more. A busted flush draggin' a fine woman down into your hole. You think you're savin' Sherman? You're damning it! You rile up the savages and buck the natural order, bringin' chaos where I brought control!"

Control.

Sharpe wanted to rule a graveyard full of quiet subjects who paid their taxes and died when he told them to. Marietta shifted her weight, pressing the butt of the rifle into her shoulder. She lined up the sights on the star: that shiny piece of tin that had lied to everyone who looked at it.

"You're done, Sharpe," Tate said. "Soon, *everyone* will know what you've done."

"And who's going to tell them?" Sharpe tilted his head. "Dead men tell no tales, son."

He raised his left hand. The trees around the barn erupted.

Men stepped around oaks and rose from behind snowdrifts. Rifle barrels emerged from the shadows like iron fingers pointing in judgment.

They'd been there the whole time—waiting, listening—as Tate walked to the gallows while Sharpe formed a noose made of words.

"Now!" Tate roared, diving to his right.

Marietta squeezed the trigger. The Winchester kicked against her shoulder as a *crack* near shattered her eardrum.

Sharpe flinched and ducked as her bullet took a chunk out of the doorframe inches from his head.

Then, the scene dissolved into fire and noise.

Gunfire exploded from the barn, the trees, and the snow. Bullets chewed the bark of the pine protecting her, sending splinters raining down into her hair. The air filled with the angry-hornet *buzz* of lead passing too close. Snow kicked up in geysers around Tate as he scrambled behind a stack of crates.

Sharpe laughed from behind the cover of a water trough—a manic, high-pitched sound that cut through the thunder of gunshots. Pointing and shouting orders, he directed his men, conducting the symphony of violence he had orchestrated.

"Pin them down! Don't let them breathe! Flank right! Get behind the girl!"

Marietta worked the lever of her rifle. *Clack-clack*. She peeked around the tree, fired blindly at a moving shape in the smoke, and ducked back as a volley shredded the wood near her ear.

Tate huddled behind the crates, but for every shot he fired, ten answered. They couldn't move or aim properly—only wait for the inevitable flank and the bullet that would find the gap in their cover.

They were trapped.

I'm sorry, Uncle.

She'd failed. She'd come here to save Fletcher and protect Tate; instead, she'd die beside him in a patch of blood-soaked snow. She closed her eyes for a second, picturing dust motes dancing in the light of her saloon, the peace she'd traded for this war.

Then, a different sound joined the chorus: the distinct *boom* of Henry rifles.

From the woods behind the barn—and the ridge *above*.

An outlaw on the barn roof spun around, his arms flailing, and toppled to the ground with a wet *thud*.

Another jerked forward as an arrow sprouted from his back, its fletching vibrating with the force of the impact.

"Take cover!" Abandoning his position by the door, Calder dove inside the barn. "They're behind us!"

It had to be Cade, Grady, and the Comanche. They hadn't run or died in the ravine, but circled back and climbed the ridge, enduring the cold, to wait for the perfect moment to strike.

"Tate!" she screamed over the din. "Move!"

Tate popped up from behind the crates, firing two quick shots that dropped an outlaw running for the trees. He sprinted toward a fallen log closer to the barn, closing the distance, flanking the outlaws—who were now pinned between two fires.

The clearing descended into absolute chaos.

Smoke from black powder hung thick and heavy, obscuring vision, turning men into ghosts. Tethered horses screamed and reared, pulling at their ropes, their eyes rolling in terror. Snow flew in blinding clouds wherever bullets struck the ground. It was a storm of man's making, more violent and unpredictable than the blizzard that had birthed it.

Marietta stepped out from behind her tree.

She didn't feel the cold anymore, nor fear, just the recoil and the smooth action of the lever as sulfur filled her nose. She saw a target. She aimed. She fired. He crumpled.

She didn't feel sick, didn't feel remorse.

She felt only the grim satisfaction of surviving.

This is what you made me, Sharpe. You made me into a killer.

To her left, movement caught her eye.

Through the swirling smoke, a low figure with a red scarf around his neck crept along the side of the barn, using the confusion to slip past Tate's line of sight. Raising a shotgun, the outlaw moved to Tate's exposed back.

No.

As Tate fumbled with the Colt's cylinder, the outlaw took aim.

Instinctively, Marietta swung her barrel, and the Winchester roared.

The outlaw jerked and fell.

Tate spun around, saw the man, then Marietta, and understood. With a quick, sharp jerk of his head, he finished loading his gun.

The shot, however, had cost her: Sharpe must have rediscovered his spine, because that shot drew his attention like a moth to flame. Ignoring the arrows raining down from the ridge, advancing gunfire from the tree line, and even his own men dying in the snow, he abandoned cover and made his way to her.

Oh, this ain't good...

Sharpe clenched his heavy Dragoon pistol in one hand. His hat had fallen off, revealing hair plastered to his skull with sweat and melted snow.

"Stupid girl!" He raised the pistol. "You shoulda stayed in the kitchen!"

Marietta pumped the lever—and froze.

Click.

She'd lost count of the rounds she'd spent saving Tate and herself. Now, staring down the barrel of Sharpe's gun, she held a useless club of wood and steel.

I'm going to die, she realized.

"Marietta!"

As Sharpe pulled the trigger with a *boom*, a shape appeared in front of Marietta and answered with return fire.

Then, the *squelch* of blood exploding into the air.

The *thud* of a heavy body hitting the ground.

The sudden grunt of air forcibly expelled from tortured lungs.

Ears ringing, Marietta looked down to see Tate sprawled on the frozen ground before her, his back turned.

"Tate?" she whispered.

He groaned.

She knelt and turned him around in her arms.

Immediately, hot, sticky warmth spread across her uncle's coat, soaking straight through the wool to drench her shirt, then seeping into her skin.

Blood—*so* much blood.

"Tate!"

Chapter Twenty-Seven

Heat radiated from the expanding red pool beneath Tate, mocking the biting chill that whipped Marietta's hair across her face. Her hands, numb and clumsy in oversized gloves, pressed against the wet wool of Tate's coat. She pushed down. *Hard.* She had to stop the flow, had to keep his life from leaking out into the indifferent snow.

He has to live.

He didn't have *permission* to die—not after yelling at her in the shed, not now that she was finally ready to admit that the empty space next to her didn't have to stay that way.

Then, his chest hitched beneath her hands.

"Get... off me... woman..."

Air rushed back into Marietta's lungs. She nearly collapsed atop him, her choked sob turning into laughter that bordered on hysterical.

"Stay down," she hissed. "You took a bullet, you mule-headed fool."

"Shoulder..." He winced, trying to shift his weight. "Just... the shoulder."

She looked closer. Blood had soaked the heavy fabric, making it look worse than a slaughterhouse floor, but the entry point sat high. Above the lung. Above the heart. The bullet had plowed a furrow through the muscle, but hadn't severed the cord that tied him to this earth.

Movement caught her eye in front of them.

Sharpe took a step backward, swaying like a pine tree caught in a gale. The heavy Dragoon pistol slipped from his fingers and struck the ice with a dull *thunk*, burying its muzzle in the snow, as he looked down at his chest.

A dark blossom unfolded on the front of his duster, right below the silver star he'd polished with such care. When he touched it, his fingers came away red.

He muttered something—maybe a name—but the wind snatched it away before it reached Marietta's ears.

Then, his knees buckled, and he folded, collapsing like a scarecrow cut from its post, and hit the ground face-first. The man who'd strangled Sherman, ordered the death of her uncle, and burned Tate's home, turned into nothing more than a heap of wet cloth and cooling meat.

The gunfire and shouting had died out. Only the wind remained, whistling through bullet holes in the barn and stirring the mane of a dead horse.

Then came the *squelch* of boots on wet snow.

Marietta grabbed her Winchester from where it had fallen, racking the lever, but a hand caught the barrel.

Cade stood over her, gently pushing the rifle muzzle toward the ground. "It's done, Marietta. It's over."

The rifle sagged as her grip failed. The weapon dropped into the snow.

Grady emerged from the trees, looking like a bear that had walked through a bramble patch. Behind him came Tamaquah, his bow held loosely in one hand. He stepped over Sharpe's body without looking down.

"Does he live?"

Tate grunted, pushing himself up to a sitting position despite Marietta's attempts to hold him down. "Takes more... than a politician with... a pop-gun... to kill me."

Cade laughed. "You look like hell, Tate."

"You ain't no prize pig yourself."

They helped Tate stand. He swayed, clutching his shoulder, but remained upright.

"Check the barn."

Grady nodded and moved toward the structure, stepping over the splintered doorframe. Cade followed, pistol drawn—just in case a rat had scurried into a dark corner.

Marietta stayed by Tate. Wrapping her arm around his waist, she took his weight on her hip. "He's gone. It's over."

Tate spat into the snow. "Good riddance."

A commotion rose inside the barn. A shout from Grady. Then, the sound of wood scraping on wood. A moment later, Grady and Cade emerged, supporting a figure between them.

Fletcher...?

He looked like raw meat. His eyes were mere slits in the doughy, purple flesh of his swollen face. His buffalo coat hung open, revealing a shirt stiff with dried blood. He dragged his feet, seemingly unable to lift them, but as they brought him into the daylight, he lifted his head.

"I told 'em..." Fletcher croaked, his voice like dry leaves crushed underfoot. "Told 'em to *go to hell.*"

Tate let out a shuddering breath. "Yeah, Fletcher, you did."

Fletcher blinked. "Ransom?"

"Dead," Cade replied. "Found him behind the water trough with an arrow in his throat."

Tamaquah nodded. "He won't burn any more lodges."

Marietta looked around the clearing. It looked like a battlefield and *smelled* like one—sulfur, copper, excrement—but the air *felt* different. Lighter. The oppressive weight hanging over Sherman, the shadow that had darkened the saloon and silenced the streets, had lifted.

The price had been high: the dead scout; Fletcher's captivity; the blood seeping from Tate's wound.

"C'mon." Grady hoisted Fletcher higher and gestured at Tate. "Let's get y'all beside a fire."

"The supply barn has a stove," Tate ventured, "and dry hay."

"No." Marietta shook her head. "We ain't stayin' in that butcher shop. We'll go back to the saloon. Nora needs to see to you two."

Cade looked at the sky. "Sun's out. We can make it to town if we ride slow."

They gathered the outlaws' mounts, figuring they'd serve well enough. Marietta helped Tate into the saddle of a roan gelding. He hissed through his teeth as his shoulder jostled, sweat beading on his upper lip, but he settled into the leather.

She mounted a mare.

They left the bodies for the coyotes and the cold. Later, perhaps someone would come back with shovels. Then again, maybe not, considering everyone's reactions to learning Sharpe's identity as the Bone Orchard Boys' mysterious leader stopped at shock. No one mentioned taking his body. Of course, the townsfolk might want to see the face of the man who'd betrayed them. Or maybe they'd just let the mountain claim its due.

Marietta didn't care either way. She never wanted to see this ravine again.

The ride back felt surreal, like a waking dream. Exhaustion settled over Marietta, a heavy blanket that dulled the edges of her vision. She watched Tate's back. He rode slumped, favoring his left side, but he didn't fall.

Tamaquah rode beside him for a while, speaking in low tones that the wind carried away. After a while, Tate offered his hand, and Tamaquah took it.

Finally, the buildings of Sherman rose from the white plains, smoke curling from their chimneys in welcoming pillars. People came out into the street as the ragged group plodded onto the main street. Old Man Miller stepped off his porch, a sack of flour in his hands. Smith lowered his hammer. Women peered from windows, clutching the shawls around their shoulders.

As Marietta pulled up in front of the saloon, the door flew open, and Nora and Adeleide rushed out.

Nora gasped. "Dear God!" She ran to Fletcher's horse. "Get him down—carefully!"

Hands reached up. Men who, only yesterday, had hidden in fear now surged forward to help ease Fletcher down, take the reins of Tate's horse, and help him dismount.

Marietta slid from her saddle.

Tate stood by the hitching rail, leaning heavily against the post. Adeleide was already fretting over him, trying to peel back his coat, but he waved her off.

As Adeleide stepped away, Marietta approached.

"I told you," she whispered, her voice thick with tears she hadn't shed. "I told you not to die."

"I listen sometimes." He offered a weak smile. "Eventually."

"Come inside. Let me clean that."

She led him into the saloon, and the familiar scents of stale beer and sawdust welcomed her like an embrace. It was warm. It was home.

They sat Tate near the fire, at the table where he and the others had planned this desperate war. Adeleide bustled in with hot water and bandages, clucking her tongue at the state of his shoulder.

Marietta poured two fingers of whiskey and set it in front of Tate.

He picked it up with a shaking hand and downed it in one swallow. The color began to creep back into his cheeks.

***

Hours passed in a blur of activity.

Nora stitched and cleaned. Fletcher got settled in the guest room again, sleeping the sleep of the not-quite-dead. The town council—Miller, Smith, and a few others—came in to hear the story. Cade told them about the ambush, the betrayal, and the fight at the barn.

He told them about Sharpe.

Marietta watched from behind the bar, cleaning glasses that weren't dirty, just to keep her hands moving.

Finally, as the sun dipped below the horizon, painting the snow in shades of violet and indigo, the crowd thinned. Cade and Grady went home, promising to return in the morning.

Tamaquah and his men had ridden back to the high country, disappearing as silently as they'd come, but not before leaving a stack of furs as a gift for the saloon.

The room quieted. Only Tate remained.

He sat by the fire, staring into the flames. His coat lay on a chair, revealing the fresh white bandage binding his shoulder. He looked weary, etched with lines of fatigue that went down to the bone, but the haunted look that had darkened his eyes since the day he walked through her door had faded.

Marietta walked around the bar, poured two mugs of coffee, and brought them to the table.

"Nora says you'll keep the arm," she murmured, "as long as you don't go chopping wood for a week."

"Nora worries too much." Tate wrapped his hands around the mug. "But she's got steady hands."

"You saved my life today, Tate."

He looked up. "You saved mine first."

A log settled in the hearth with a soft crumble of ash. Tate took a slow sip from his mug, dropping his shoulders an inch. The air between them no longer vibrated with words unsaid or debts unpaid; it held only the scent of roasted beans and woodsmoke.

"What will you do now?" she asked. "Your ranch is... well, it's still a ruin."

"Foundation's good." He traced the rim of the mug. "Land's still there. Soil's still deep. A man can build a lot on a good foundation."

"You aim to rebuild, then?"

"I do."

He set the mug down. Then, he looked at the map on the wall, filled with circles and dead ends. Finally, he looked at her.

"But a house ain't a home just 'cause it has walls, Marietta."

Her heart gave an uneven thump against her ribs. "No. Reckon it ain't."

He stood up, wincing slightly as his shoulder moved, but he pushed through it. He walked around the table and stopped beside her chair, then held out his hand.

She took it.

"I've spent fourteen years lookin' backward," he said. "Lookin' at graves. Lookin' at ash. I forgot what it was like to look forward."

"And what do you see now?"

"I see *you*."

He pulled her up gently. She stood close to him, smelling the soap Nora had used to wash the blood from his skin and the lingering scent of woodsmoke.

"I ain't a man of means," he said. "My cattle are gone. My barn is charcoal. I come with scars, Marietta. Inside and out."

"We all got scars, Tate." She reached up, touching the bandage on his shoulder. "Shows we survived."

"I don't want to just *survive* anymore." He looked into her eyes. "I want to *live*. I want to plant crops and watch 'em grow. I want to sit on a porch and watch the sun go down without waitin' for a gunshot. And I don't want to do any of it alone."

Marietta's breath caught.

"You stood by me in the fire," he continued. "You walked into a blizzard for me. You're the bravest, most stubborn, most beautiful woman God ever put on this earth."

He squeezed her hand.

"Marietta Walker, would you do a broken-down rancher the honor of being his wife?"

Marietta smiled, and a tear tracked a hot line down her cheek as her thoughts wandered to Uncle Everett. He would've grumbled about Tate's lack of assets while admiring the man's spine. He'd have liked how Tate looked at her.

"You ain't broken, Tate," she whispered. "Just a little battered."

"Is that a yes?"

"Yes." She laughed. "Yes, you fool. Yes!"

He leaned down and kissed her.

It wasn't like their first two kisses. This was slow. Deliberate. A promise sealed in breath and touch. It tasted of coffee and hope, of a future that hadn't existed yesterday.

Eventually, he pulled back and rested his forehead against hers.

"We got a lot of work to do," he murmured.

"The saloon needs fixin'."

"My fences are down."

"The town needs healin'."

Marietta looked over his shoulder, out the window, where the frost was beginning to melt. The streetlights of Sherman flickered on, one by one, casting golden pools on the snow. The silver star was gone, yet the darkness had retreated.

A star in the darkness... Wait—what day is it?

With a start, she realized it was Christmas Eve.

"Merry Christmas, Tate," she whispered.

He smiled. "Merry Christmas, Marietta."

Epilogue

Sherman, Texas, Christmas 1868

One year later

The hammer struck the nail with a ringing *thwack* that vibrated through the pine board and traveled straight up Tate's arm.

Stepping back, he admired the mistletoe he'd just fastened to the support beam above the cast-iron stove. White berries shone like pearls against dark green leaves, contrasting the rough-hewn timber of the ceiling. Heat rolled off the black iron stove, carrying the scent of roasting ham and glazing sugar, filling the kitchen with a richness that made his stomach growl.

A year ago, this room had smelled of charred wood and wet ash.

Now, it smelled of life.

"Tate Hollister, if you don't get that weed away from my fire *this* instant, I will scald your hide 'til it ain't worth tanning."

Tate turned, hiding the grin that tugged at his beard.

Marietta stood in the doorway to the main room, wiping her hands on a flour-dusted apron that stretched tight over the swell of her belly. Her green eyes flashed with mock severity, though their corners crinkled with suppressed amusement.

He slid the hammer into his tool belt. "You got a heart harder than a hickory knot, woman. Where's your Christmas spirit?"

"I got plenty of spirit—just don't fancy burnin' the roof down around our ears 'fore the ham's even sweated." She waddled toward him. "You hang dry leaves above a hot stove, you're askin' for it. Sparks hit dry leaves, and *poof*—no Christmas dinner."

"It ain't dry," he protested. "Cut it fresh this mornin'."

"Move it." She brandished a wooden spoon at the doorway. "Put it over the threshold like folks with sense."

He held up his hands in surrender. "Yes, ma'am."

He climbed back up the step stool, pried the nail loose with the claw of his hammer, and moved the decoration to the archway. As he worked, he watched her out of the corner of his eye.

She moved to the stove, lifted the heavy lid of a pot, and stirred the mashed potatoes with vigorous strokes. Steam billowed around her, curling dark tendrils of hair that had escaped her bun. Her skin captured the flush of heat.

She glowed; not in the poetic sense the books in the mercantile talked about, but in a visceral way that hit Tate in the gut. She carried his child, a life they'd made in the quiet months after the guns fell silent, and the sight of her filled hollow places inside him that he'd thought would remain empty forever.

"Door!" Cade Avery kicked the front door with his boot heel. "Open up before my fingers snap off!"

Tate jumped down and crossed the main room, then threw the heavy bolt and swung the oak door wide. A gust of wind swirled into the room, bringing snowflakes to dance briefly in the firelight before melting on the floorboards.

Cade and Grady staggered in, their arms loaded with split logs. Snow dusted their hats and shoulders, turning them into white-capped mountains.

"Shut it! Shut it!" Cade dropped his load into the wood box with a thunderous *crash*. "Air's bitin' harder than a cornered rattler out there."

Grady followed, placing his logs with considerably more care. "Aw, quit your bellyachin'. Ain't nothin' but a brisk breeze."

Tate pushed the door shut. "You two squawk worse than a pair of wet hens."

Cade stripped off his gloves and blew into his cupped hands. "That's rich, comin' from a man who's been tastin' gravy all afternoon."

"Someone's gotta keep an eye on the cook."

"Is that right?" Marietta called from the kitchen. "Keep talkin' like that, Hollister, and you'll be keepin' an eye on the horses while they eat *their* Christmas dinner!"

Cade grinned, clapping Tate on the shoulder. "See? Marriage suits you."

Nora appeared from the back room, carrying a stack of folded napkins. She wore a dress of deep blue wool and a matching ribbon in her hair. She and Cade had tied the knot in the spring.

"Leave him be, Cade." She pecked her husband on the cheek. "Tate's just tryin' to make everything perfect."

Tate looked around the room.

The walls stood solid, built of timber Tate had felled and planed with his own hands. The fireplace, constructed from river stones he and Marietta had gathered, blazed with cheerful flames that chased the shadows into the corners. A fir tree stood in the corner, decorated with strings of popcorn, dried berries, and stars cut from old coffee cans.

Grady accepted a mug of cider from Nora. "How's the herd?"

"Good." Tate leaned against the mantel. "Frost took a calf last week, but the rest are huddled in the lower canyon. The stored feed in the new barn is holdin' out."

"And the neighbors?"

"Quiet." Tate took a sip from his own mug. "A patrol from Tamaquah's band crossed the north ridge yesterday. Left a stack of cured hides by the fence."

Cade whistled low. "Still find it hard to believe. Two years ago, we'd have been reachin' for our rifles."

"Things change." Tate looked at the rug in front of the hearth, a thick buffalo hide Tamaquah had gifted them at the wedding. "Men change. If they got sense."

After last Christmas, the Bone Orchard Boys had shattered like glass under a hammer. Without Sharpe to guide them and Calder to drive them, the gang's remnants had scattered to the winds, running for the territories or Mexico. Sherman had breathed again.

The sheriff's badge now sat in a drawer in the mayor's desk, awaiting a man worthy enough to pin it on.

"Grub's up!" Marietta said from the kitchen. "And if you men don't wash your hands, you don't get no biscuits!"

They moved to the table.

Tate sat at the head. Marietta sat to his right, struggling slightly to lower herself into the chair. Cade and Nora took one side, Grady the other.

The table groaned under the weight of the feast.

The ham, glazed with honey and cloves, sat like a king on a platter. Bowls of potatoes, candied yams, preserved green beans from the summer garden, and a basket of biscuits steaming in the cool air filled every inch of space.

"Tate?" Marietta nodded at the food. "You gonna say grace?"

He cleared his throat and bowed his head.

"Lord..." He paused, searching for words. The old prayers, about deliverance and protection, didn't seem appropriate. "We thank You for this food. We thank You for the roof over our heads and the fire in the hearth. We thank You for friends who stand by us in the storm and sit with us in the calm."

Marietta's hand slipped into his.

"We ask Your blessing on this house," he continued, his voice thickening, "and on the new life comin' into it. Let us raise him—or her—to know the value of dirt, the strength of truth, and the peace we found here. Amen."

"*Amen*," the table echoed.

Knives clattered against plates. Pitchers poured. Laughter rose and fell like the tide.

Later, after the pies—apple and pumpkin—had been demolished and the coffee pot emptied twice, the lethargy of full bellies and a warm room settled over them.

Grady stretched. "Reckon I best head out. Sarah gets cross if I ain't home to read the Christmas story before bed."

"Ride careful," Tate said. "Snow's starting to stick."

"Always do."

Cade stood up, helping Nora with her shawl. "We'll head out too. You two have fun."

The process of leaving took time—finding coats, wrapping scarves, exchanging hugs. Marietta held Nora for a long moment, whispering something that made both women giggle. Tate shook Cade's hand.

"Merry Christmas, Tate."

"Merry Christmas, Cade."

Then, the door opened and closed, letting in a brief swirl of cold before sealing Tate and Marietta in again.

Marietta moved around the room, gathering plates.

"Leave it," Tate said. "I'll wash up in the morning."

"Don't sit right leaving a mess on Christmas."

"Sit." He guided her to the armchair by the fire. "You've been on your feet since dawn."

She sank into the cushion with a sigh of relief. "My ankles feel like tree trunks."

Tate knelt before her and unlaced her boots, sliding them off one by one. He rubbed her feet, his thumbs working their arches, feeling the tension melt away from her frame.

She leaned her head back, eyes closing, a hum of contentment escaping her lips. "You spoil me, Tate Hollister."

"Just protectin' my investment." Smiling, he winked up at her. "Can't have the foreman goin' lame on me."

She opened one eye. "Foreman? I *own* half this operation."

"That you do."

He stood and walked to the wood box, throwing another log onto the fire. "I need some air."

"Take a coat. It's freezing."

"Be back in a minute."

He grabbed his heavy wool coat from its peg and stepped out onto the porch.

Inhaling deeply, he let the icy air scour his lungs. Snow fell softly, fat flakes drifting down in the windless night to cover the scars of the land. The burned foundation of the old barn lay buried under a foot of pristine white. Further up the slope, the new barn stood proudly against the tree line.

He leaned against the porch railing.

A year ago, he'd been shivering in a shed, waiting for a bullet. He'd been a man defined by loss, carrying the ghosts of his parents, Wyatt, and Lynda like stones in a sack, dragging them with him every step.

Marietta stepped onto the porch. She'd wrapped a thick woolen shawl around her shoulders, pulling it tight over her belly. She didn't speak, simply moved to his side, and leaned against him.

He wrapped his arm around her, pulling her into the shelter of his coat.

"You'll catch cold," he murmured.

"The fire was too warm." She rested her head on his shoulder. "Needed to see the snow."

They watched it fall together.

"It's beautiful," she said.

"It is."

"Last year... I thought snow was the devil's blanket. Thought it would bury us all."

"It tried." Tate tightened his grip on her. "But we dug out."

"Do you still think about it?" She looked up at him, her breath misting in the air. "The ravine? Sharpe?"

"Less and less."

He looked down at her face, serene and pale in the moonlight. The hardness that had defined her in the saloon, the brittle strength she'd worn like armor, had resolved into something more resilient. She wasn't iron anymore; she was willow. She could bend without breaking.

"I was scared today," he said.

"Why?"

"When I looked around that table. I saw everything I ever wanted—everything I thought I'd never have again—and fear hit me... that the sky would fall. That God would realize He'd made a mistake, giving a man like me this much joy."

Marietta turned in his arms, then reached up, framing his face with her hands. The wool of her shawl scratched against his neck.

"You earned this. *We* earned this." She pressed her forehead to his. "Besides, I don't think He'd give us all this just to take it away."

He closed his eyes, breathing her scent.

"The baby kicked," she whispered.

His eyes snapped open. "Now?"

"Just a flutter. Like a butterfly wing."

He moved his hand to her belly and waited. Cold seeped through his coat, but the heat radiating from her centered him. Then, he felt it: a tiny yet distinct thump against his palm.

A laugh bubbled up in his chest. "Strong. Like his daddy."

"Or stubborn. Like his mama."

"Probably both." He shook his head and chuckled. "Lord help us."

THE END

Also by Zachary McCrae

Thanks for ridin' along with "**The Texas Blizzard**"!

If it hit the mark for you, you can find more of my stories right here:

https://go.zacharymccrae.com/bc-authorpage

Thank you kindly!

Made in United States
Troutdale, OR
12/02/2025

42946859R00136